THE DOOR IN THE ALLEY

THE EXPLORERS

THE DOOR IN THE ALLEY

ADRIENNE KRESS

Illustrated by Matthew C. Rockefeller

DELACORTE PRESS

Text copyright © 2017 by Adrienne Kress
Jacket art and interior illustrations copyright © 2017 by Matthew C. Rockefeller

All rights reserved. Published in the United States by Delacorte Press, an imprint of Random House Children's Books, a division of Penguin Random House LLC, New York.

Delacorte Press is a registered trademark and the colophon is a trademark of Penguin Random House LLC.

Visit us on the Web! randomhousekids.com

Educators and librarians, for a variety of teaching tools, visit us at RHTeachersLibrarians.com

Library of Congress Cataloging-in-Publication Data is available upon request.
ISBN 978-1-101-94005-1 (trade) — ISBN 978-1-101-94006-8 (lib. bdg.) — ISBN 978-1-101-94007-5 (ebook)

The text of this book is set in 12-point Sabon.
Interior design by Michelle Gengaro

Printed in the United States of America
10 9 8 7 6 5 4 3 2 1
First Edition

Random House Children's Books supports the First Amendment and celebrates the right to read.

To the usual suspects.
And also the unusual ones.

CHAPTER 1

In which we meet Sebastian.

This story begins, like most stories do, with a pig wearing a teeny hat. And I'm sure right now you're thinking to yourself, *I've read this story before.* But please let me assure you that this isn't *that* pig in a teeny hat story you're reading, but the other one. The one you haven't read. Yet.

Unless you've read this story before.

And also, I'm lying. I must confess that this story doesn't literally begin with a pig wearing a teeny hat, but figuratively does. This story actually begins with Sebastian coming home from school. Because that's a pretty regular thing that Sebastian did, school being a regular thing that one does when one is twelve.

Well, okay, I guess technically this story began with

me telling you it begins with a pig in a teeny hat, but let's pretend that it began with Sebastian coming home from school.

Yes?

Excellent.

So, this story begins with Sebastian coming home from school.

Sebastian had to take the Y train and the number 42 and the Blue Express to get to and from school. He also had to walk for twenty minutes. It wasn't that his school was across the country or anything, but the city he lived in was really big. And he went to a special school that happened to be far away from where he lived. It was for grades four to eight and focused on math and the sciences. Sebastian, you see, had always been rather good at math and science.

It wasn't really that surprising that he was. As he had learned, thanks to science, his skills had kind of been hardwired into his DNA from the beginning. Both his parents worked at the university in the physics department. His older brother was studying to be an actuary,[1] and his brother's twin sister was already an accomplished engineer who specialized in bridges.

---

[1] Funny thing, no one actually knows what an actuary does, not even actuaries. Some have speculated that's where the name comes from: "What do you do?" "Actually, I have no idea."

It was a family of pragmatic minds, and Sebastian fit in perfectly. He was able to contribute to conversations around the dinner table and was equally as amused as his parents and brother and sister were by the usual math- and science-related jokes told during their meals together. He was happy in his family, happy in his school, and sure about his place in the world and his future on the planet. He had the goal of being a neurosurgeon when he grew up. And, yes, his cousin and best friend, Arthur, teased him about being a zombie: "Brains! Brains!" But that was okay—he felt confident that his life choices were wise and good ones.

He was equally as confident that the path he took every day to and from school was wise and good. It was the quickest and most efficient, and what could be wiser and . . . gooder . . . than that? The trains and buses he chose were not only the ones with the fewest stops, but also the ones with the least amount of walking distance between transfers. And the walk from the station to school was by far the shortest route.

But Arthur. Oh, Arthur. Arthur, though Sebastian's cousin, had a recklessness to him. It was probably what interested Sebastian most in his friend, and what frustrated him most as well. And it was, obviously, Arthur who messed everything up.

On the day that changed it all, Arthur had accompanied Sebastian back to his house. This happened on occasion, though always with a quick call home to Sebastian's parents, of course, to confirm that such spontaneity would be welcome. Arthur was generally a lot of fun to be around, but that day he was a little grumpy. He had gotten a C on his biology exam and was in a ranting kind of mood.

"I think Mrs. Brown just has it in for me."

Sebastian had kept quiet for most of the rant, but this was getting ridiculous. "That makes no sense."

"What?" Arthur asked, clearly surprised at the interruption.

"Well, did she grade your paper wrong? Were there questions you got right that she said you didn't?"

Arthur stopped walking. Sebastian sighed. He stopped walking too. He glanced at his watch, which was the kind of watch that you set by a satellite and therefore is never wrong. Stopping was not part of the getting-home-efficiently plan.

"You could be on my side, you know," said Arthur, his lower lip twitching so subtly that Sebastian wouldn't have noticed it had he not accidentally been staring right at it.

"I'm not *not* on your side," Sebastian answered honestly.

"Well, you're not *not* not on my side either."

"I just don't understand how she has it in for you."

"Oh, for . . . You know what, Sebastian? Never mind."

And then Arthur did something that was truly shocking. He turned down the wrong street. It was the street that ran parallel to the correct street, the street that in two more turns would take them directly to Sebastian's front door. This street, Sebastian had observed back when he'd been mapping out his route at home, was not a good street. This street wasn't even really a street. It was a dead end. It would mean they'd have to walk up it and then back down it again.

A complete waste of time.

"Arthur, come on!" Sebastian called out after him.

But it was too late.

Oh, how too late it was.

He could have continued home on his own, but Sebastian knew that was the wrong move to make at a time like this. His cousin was upset, and Sebastian was a good friend, so, reconciled to the waste of time, he followed Arthur.

This street was very similar to the correct street. Terraced brownstones lined both sides, wrought-iron gates kept trespassers at bay, and leafy green-turning-gold trees canopied overhead. Arthur was almost two-thirds of the way down the street, and Sebastian had to jog to catch up.

"I'm sorry," he said when he did.

"Yeah?" Arthur stopped and glared at him. "For what?"

"For . . ." Darn. Arthur knew him too well. "Okay, I don't know what for."

"Yeah. I know."

"Can we just forget all this and go home?"

Arthur stood silently for a moment. And then he nodded. "Would be nice if you had my back once in a while, though."

Sebastian was thrown by that comment. "I do."

"Yeah, not really. You always take . . . logic's side." Arthur continued up the street.

Sebastian personally considered that a compliment, though the way Arthur said it, it was clearly not meant to be taken as one. But he didn't really have time to process what he was supposed to feel. Instead he called out: "Hey! You can't go that way, there's a dead end!"

"No, there's an alley up ahead. I can see it."

There was? Sebastian was surprised—he hadn't noticed an alley when he'd set his route, but he shrugged and kept walking. An alley would make up some much-needed time.

Sure enough, as Sebastian caught up with Arthur, he could see that his cousin was right. There was indeed a dark, narrow alley that opened up onto the street they needed to get back on their path. Sebastian felt a wave of relief and happily ventured into the dark shadows.

Of course for some people, this would have been a slightly scary prospect. Alleys in general tend to have an air of mystery that can be awfully ostentatious[2] but this alley in particular was, well, for want of a better word, creepy.

"Kind of creepy," said Arthur from behind him.

Sebastian pulled some small comfort from his vast armory of logic. "It's just dark because the walls block out the sun. Don't be scared."

"I'm not scared," Arthur said, but it was clear to Sebastian that the words were meaningless.

So Sebastian tried to make him feel better. "First of all, the street is right there," he told his cousin, pointing to the other side of the alley. "Second, chances are no one ever comes here. It'd be different if we were downtown, but this is a residential street. No one has any reason to hang out back here."

"Yeah, well, what about them?"

---

[2] *Though they remain not nearly as pretentious as culs-de-sac.*

Sebastian turned and looked to where Arthur was pointing. On the red brick wall beside a door he hadn't even noticed was a plaque. It read:

Sebastian shrugged. "Okay, I guess the people who belong to the society come here. But that's not scary."

"It's not?" Arthur looked at him warily.

"What's scary about explorers?"

Arthur had no answer, and so they continued on down the alley. They came out on the other side, connected with Sebastian's regular route, and walked the rest of the way home, unfortunately arriving at his house five minutes later than normal. Arthur stayed until dinnertime, when he decided to go home after a fruitful afternoon of helping Sebastian map out another third of the dark side of the moon.

Yes, after all the excitement, it had turned into an altogether average day. That is to say, on the surface. Sebastian, though, was not feeling remotely average at all. No matter how hard he pretended he was—and indeed pretended so well that Arthur was none the wiser—he couldn't pretend well enough to fool himself.

The thing was that Sebastian, ever since he'd seen it, had been attempting to put the sign for The Explorers Society out of his head. He attempted to do it over dinner when he asked for the "society" of ketchup instead of "bottle." He attempted to do it when he asked if they could watch a show on the Explorer channel. And he attempted to do it lying awake that night, staring at his ceiling, which was covered with an accurate map of the stars for that time of year. All he saw in his mind's eye was that strange sign with those words: The Explorers Society.

Try as he might, he couldn't shake that sign. Of course, it wasn't the sign itself that disturbed him so, though he did find its font rather impractical. It was what the sign meant. While it seemed to be obvious, Sebastian simply refused to believe that it was possible that it meant what he thought it meant. Who actually did that for a job? Surely there was no living to be made being an explorer. Surely everything had already been explored.

He figured the sign had to mean something else altogether. Maybe it was a society full of people with the last name Explorer. Or maybe they had neglected to add an apostrophe before the *s* and there was just one explorer and this was his or her society. That made more sense to him. He could conceive of one reckless person choosing to be an explorer. But many?

It was simply too far-fetched.

You might wonder why it got to him like this. After all, there are many other signs out there that can be equally puzzling.[3] But, no, it was this particular sign and the words written on it that had captured him. And it was likely not about the word "Society" or the "The" either. Those two words he'd seen often. In fact, he saw the word "the" several times a day. No. It was the word "Explorers" that was gnawing away at him. It was as if the word had awoken something deep within him, and it scared him a little. See, the thing was, he found the word "Explorers" rather . . . exciting. And he just did not consider it appropriate to feel like that about that particular word.

Sebastian wondered, could he be experiencing his first identity crisis at twelve years old? It was impossible to say, as he'd never had one before to compare it to, yet as he went to school the next day he felt utterly

---

[3] Like: Do Not Enter (why would someone put a door there, then?) or Back in Five (Five what, I ask you. Five what?).

miserable. So miserable that he raised his hand to answer questions only sixteen times.

As the clock ominously ticked down the minutes of the day,[4] Sebastian's stomach got tighter and tighter. He knew he could avoid the sign if he chose. All he had to do was follow his usual route home. As a further precaution, he made sure Arthur had no interest in coming over. After all, it had been Arthur and his reckless behavior that had started all this. The thing was, for the first time, possibly ever, Sebastian didn't trust himself. He just didn't know if he could make it all the way home without choosing to look at the sign again. He really needed to get this sign out of his head.

Soon enough it was the end of the day and soon enough Sebastian found himself on the 42 attempting to calm his breathing and clear his mind, and then on the Blue Express dreading the inevitable arrival at his stop. And when finally he was walking that last dreaded stretch home, he clenched his hands into fists and tried everything he could to feel, or at least give the impression of *looking*, totally and completely normal.

Sebastian followed his regular route and every step

---

[4] That had nothing to do with how Sebastian was feeling, by the way—the clock in his classroom just happened to tick ominously. Just as the clock down the hall in 4B ticked reluctantly, and the clock in the principal's office ticked appreciatively.

he took closer to the wrong street made him more and more miserable. His regular route took him right past it, and he just had to walk by, he had to ignore it. When he was finally crossing the street he made a concerted effort not to look up toward the alley. He even held his breath. And then he was across and turning up the correct street. A heavy weight lifted off his shoulders, and for the first time that day, Sebastian smiled.

And that's when it happened.

The pig in the teeny hat.

➤ CHAPTER 2 ◄

In which we meet a pig
in a teeny hat.

It is a truth universally acknowledged that a teeny hat on an animal is hilarious. Because animals don't wear hats. People do. And also hats being teeny on the teeny heads of animals make it look as if they were made for them and thus make it seem as if the animals like to dress up fancy.

You might happen to occasionally see an animal wearing a teeny hat in a photograph, and maybe at Halloween you'll see an animal whose owner dressed it in a costume that includes a hat. Like a pirate. But how often do you see an animal, on its own, out in the wild, wearing a hat?[5]

---

[5] I mean, that would be really weird, wouldn't it, if one day let's say a bird landed on the wire by your bedroom window and he was wearing a fedora? It would also be weird if he had an old-

Anyway, the point is, while we sometimes see animals in teeny hats and find it amusing, we don't often see one unattended. That is to say, without a human present. Because that makes no sense. And let me tell you, Sebastian did not find it funny when he saw the pig in the teeny hat. First of all, because, as I said, it made no sense, and when things made no sense Sebastian got uncomfortable. But also because it was a pig. And you just don't see that many pigs in the city, fewer still wearing teeny hats.

The pig was small, maybe around elementary school pig age, and had a panicked look in its eyes. It was jogging down the sidewalk right in Sebastian's path. And when it noticed Sebastian coming directly for it, its expression turned from panic to pure terror. It looked left, then right, and then, determining that its life was in immediate danger, ran out into the street.

Working purely off an instinct he didn't even know he had, Sebastian launched himself after the pig, picking it up in his arms and rushing to the other side of

fashioned camera and spoke like a 1940s reporter. Because you don't want anyone taking pictures of you through your window. That's intrusive.

the street just before a minivan whooshed past. He held the pig tight in his arms, panting a little, and looked down at it. The pig still looked petrified, its hat now askew, but for some reason it didn't struggle. Instead it seemed just to resign itself quietly to this moment of sheer terror, and froze.

"My pig!" called out a voice, and Sebastian turned to see a man fly out of the alley and into the street, much in the same way the pig had. The man wore a tweed suit, but the jacket was unbuttoned and flapping about as he ran. His hair was white, and tufts sprouted

from different parts of his head without any consideration for symmetry. And he ran not in a straight line across the street, but in a zigzag fashion, so that despite the man's fluster and panic, he took quite a while to succeed in crossing the street.

Finally he arrived to where Sebastian stood holding the pig, and he doubled over, panting hard. He placed his hands on his thighs and looked up for a moment as if he was going to speak, then bent over again, holding up a hand indicating he needed another moment before he could say anything. Sebastian and the pig just watched him as he did this several times, attempting to speak but not speaking. And finally Sebastian thought maybe he should be the one to talk first.

"Sir . . . ," he started, but the man held up his finger, giving an extra-loud wheeze. "Sir, I . . ." The man poked the air hard with his finger as if to make sure Sebastian was aware of its presence. So Sebastian fell silent and looked down at the pig again. The pig looked up at him, still terrified but now seeming also mildly confused.

Finally the man straightened himself and, removing the pocket square from his jacket, wiped his forehead and sighed. Then he said, "That's my pig."

"Yes, I gathered that," replied Sebastian. "Would

you like him back?" He stretched out his arms, but the man took a step backward.

"Oh, no no no. No. No." He pressed his lips together. "Yes."

"Okay . . . so here." Sebastian took a step toward him.

"No no no no. No. You must bring him. He's never this still when I hold him. No. I can't take him. He'll just run away again."

Sebastian slowly brought the pig back to his chest. "How long will this take?"

"What? What do you mean by that?" The man stared at him as if offended. "How insensitive! How . . . Oh. 'How long will this take?' Not long. Not long at all. I'm just around the corner." He gestured to Sebastian to follow him, which clearly Sebastian couldn't reasonably do as walking in a zigzag went against everything he believed in. Instead he walked across the street as the man made his jagged journey to the other side. The man bent over again to catch his breath in wheezing gulps.

"Why don't you just walk in a straight line?" asked Sebastian, feeling a little concerned for the old man's health.

When the man stood upright again he gave Sebastian

a look and said slowly, "I don't see what that would accomplish."

"Uh . . . getting to places faster?" replied Sebastian just as slowly.

"And what is the point of that?"

They stared at each other, and Sebastian had an odd feeling that the man was finding Sebastian just as bizarre as he was finding the man.

"Maybe we should just get this pig back to wherever," said Sebastian finally. The man nodded, gave him one more look, and turned slowly. And suddenly he was off zigzagging, and Sebastian had to just stand there and watch until the man finally went where he was trying to go.

That's when Sebastian's heart sank.

In all the confusion, with the pig and the teeny hat and the zigzag man, he had completely forgotten about the thing he had been trying to forget about. In one way, it meant he had done an excellent job at avoiding it up until now; in another, it meant that his guard had been down. For, sure enough, the man had turned down an alley. The only alley that existed on this street. That connected to another street. And there was only one thing down that alley.

Sebastian approached it with caution, his expression slowly morphing into the one the pig had been wearing all this time. Terror. He stood at the end of the dark passageway and peeked his head around the corner only to see the man standing right by the door. And right under the sign that read . . .

The Explorers Society

"Come on come on come on. He is a pig, after all," called out the man, opening the door.

"What does that even mean?" Sebastian called back.

"It means . . . he is a pig." Once more the man gave him that look.

Fine, thought Sebastian. The sooner he followed him the sooner it would be over. He took in a deep breath, squeezed the pig close, and made his way down the dark alley to the man and through the door he held open for him. The man followed, closing the door behind him.

Sebastian found himself standing in a small dark foyer, no larger than a midsized elevator, with the strange man at his side. The walls were paneled with dark wood, and a long staircase loomed before them, carpeted with a dark red, almost black, runner. A single dusty lightbulb dangled from the ceiling.

"Going up!" announced the man. And suddenly

they *were*. Going up. The floor and walls and light stayed around him, but the staircase fell away as they rose in what had turned out to be an actual elevator—one that happened to be missing a few of its walls.

They traveled upward, rushing past floor after floor of oddities. Sebastian only caught glimpses, but from what he could see there were statues, a room of mirrors, something furry. They kept going and going, and Sebastian was certain they'd have to reach the top eventually. Wouldn't they? And just when he was sure they would go crashing through the roof, they came to a sudden stop. In what appeared to be exactly the same space as before, though Sebastian was well aware that wasn't logical.

Sebastian followed the man forward and glanced at the stairs as they walked past them. "Where do those stairs go?"

"What stairs?" replied the man, turning a corner and leading them down a dark hall, the walls of which were covered in empty picture frames.

"The stairs back there." Sebastian glanced back.

"Those aren't stairs."

Sebastian blinked. "They aren't?"

"No. We showcase a series of life-sized paintings of stairs here at the society headquarters. It's called 'Up and Down.' Each one has a slightly different ratio of height to width meant to express the inner turmoil one feels at the foot of a staircase. You thought they were real?"

"Yes. . . ." Confusion coiled itself around Sebastian's brain and squeezed. Obviously he had thought they were real, otherwise he wouldn't have asked the question.

The man let out a blustery laugh. "They don't even look real! Stairs don't look like that."

Sebastian's brain was now being strangled. "Actually they look exactly like that."

"Son, you might be good with pigs in hats, but you are clearly not very bright."

Sebastian wanted to respond to that pronouncement that certainly he'd been called many things in his life—"too serious," "ahead of the curve," "Sebastian" (his parents didn't believe in nicknames)—but "not very bright" had never been one of them. Instead, though, all he could do was sputter as the man flung open a door. The hall flooded with bright pink light, which Sebastian learned, upon stepping through into the room, was caused by a massive neon sign of an ampersand.[6]

---

[6] Okay, so here's the thing: "ampersand" means this: &. That is to say, it is the name for the symbol that represents the word

"What's that?" asked Sebastian, staring at it in awe. He was so stunned by it that he was barely able to take in the rest of the room, noticing only briefly all the animal cages (from within which squawks and squeaks could be heard) as well as the long table full of hatmaking supplies.

"Enough!" barked the man, violently grabbing the pig out of Sebastian's arms. The pig erupted into a fit of ear-piercing squeals and flailed its pig legs about, struggling to get free. The man fought his way across the room to a large pen tucked into the far corner. "Your questions are ridiculous!"

No, they aren't, thought Sebastian, feeling more hurt than he understood was reasonable. He had always prided himself on asking really good questions. He quickly analyzed the questions he'd been asking and acknowledged that, yes, maybe he should have been more specific, but hadn't it been kind of obvious what he was referring to? He stayed lost in his thoughts until a short round woman with tight curls of gray hair came barging into the room.

"Where is David Copperfield?"

Sebastian was sure that was a way worse question

"and." So why is it "ampersand" and not "and-ersand," I ask you? Why??

than the one he'd just asked. But instead of reprimand-
ing this woman, the man looked scared. He flashed a
nervous smile and didn't say a thing. Sebastian found
his reaction both amusing and satisfying. It was nice
finally getting to see the man as flustered as he felt.

"I asked you a question, Hubert!" said the woman,
her hands on her hips and her eyes narrowing.

"I, um, I . . ."

"So help me, Hubert, if I see so much as a brim of
a little hat . . ."

"No, no, no. There were no hats involved!"

A soft echoey meow came from somewhere near
Sebastian's ankle. He glanced down and saw a calico
cat, its tail sticking straight up
into the air, with what looked
to be a miniature knight's
helmet hiding its head.

The woman slowly
pointed at the cat, never
breaking eye contact with
Hubert.

"That's not a little hat!"
he protested, his voice cracking. "It's a little *helmet*!"

"Take that off him this instant!"

Hubert looked perfectly defeated. He crossed over

to Sebastian and bent to pick up the cat. He glanced at the woman, and then sighed deeply, removing the helmet from the cat's head. The cat looked at Sebastian with an expression that was a cross between amused and annoyed, and then hopped out of Hubert's arms and trotted to the woman's side.

"You!" she said when she had given the cat a good scratch behind the ears—to which the cat responded enthusiastically. "You!" she said again.

"Me?" asked Sebastian, startled and a little unsure whether she did indeed mean him.

"Yes. Are you a friend of Hubert's?"

"Uh, not really."

"Excellent. Come with me. It's time for tea."

➤ CHAPTER 3 ◄

In which . . . tea.

For some reason that escaped him (for there simply had to be one somewhere), Sebastian dutifully followed the woman out of the pink-lit room and into the hallway. He followed her back the way he'd come until they were once again facing the painting of the ascending stairs. With barely a pause the woman grabbed hold of the side of the painting and pulled on its frame, opening up what was evidently not a painting, exactly, but a painted door, and started up the stairs that had been hidden behind it.

Sebastian stopped and looked at the staircase with suspicion, watching as the woman climbed quickly and disappeared into the darkness beyond. He glanced down and noticed David Copperfield looking at him with an equal amount of suspicion. They stared at each other for a moment. "Okay, okay," he said. And he started up the stairs.

It was a long staircase. And just as Sebastian was wondering if he might wind up climbing for the rest of his life, he found himself walking into a warm natural light. When Sebastian's eyes adjusted to it he saw an open door at the very top of the stairs. He continued his climb until he reached the top; then he stepped through the opening and stared. He was standing on a rooftop terrace with a truly magnificent 360-degree view of the city. Flowers were everywhere, in pots and boxed planters, but they also seemed to sprout out of the roof itself. They poured onto a cobblestone pathway that led to a large expanse of thick glass. Sebastian stopped where it began. In the middle of the glass patio grew a large tree. Or rather, what appeared to be the *top* of a large tree—Sebastian could swear it looked as if the tree continued down through the roof, into the society itself. And as Sebastian tentatively approached the edge of the glass floor and looked down through it, he was pretty sure that was exactly what it did.

The tree stretched down through the building to what Sebastian could only guess was the ground floor of The Explorers Society. He looked up at its branches,

which reached into the sky and caught his breath. Sitting above him in the tree's leafy canopy was, for want of a better word, a tree house. It wasn't much more than a platform—it had no roof or railings—but it was certainly built to be climbed into and sat upon. It was made of what looked like a rich cherry wood and had a rope ladder hanging from each of its four sides.

Sebastian inched closer over the glass rooftop and the words of the woman he'd followed began to make slightly more sense. He could see that on the tree house platform there was a table covered with a fine white tablecloth along with two wrought-iron seats painted white, with pale blue cushions. The woman was sitting in one of these chairs, looking at him with obvious impatience. Before her was a full tea service: teapot, cups, saucers, milk and sugar, and a three-tiered display of little cakes and sandwiches. All of which Sebastian discerned as he tentatively climbed a rope ladder up to the platform.

David Copperfield bypassed the ladders and climbed the tree.

"Please have a seat," said the woman.

Once again, without quite understanding why, Sebastian did as he was told.

"I've already poured us two cups." She waved her hands over two cups of steaming tea, each sitting on a little matching saucer. The saucers in turn matched the floral teapot that sat next to the cakes and sandwiches. It was all so . . . perfect.

"Oh yeah, you have," said Sebastian, staring into his cup and wondering how she'd known to have tea prepared for him when she'd only just met him and when she'd had time to pour him a cup of tea and why he cared so much about the pouring of tea into cups in the first place.

"Milk? Sugar?"

Sebastian shrugged. Maybe. Maybe not. He'd never had tea before. He thought it strange to create something that was incomplete. If tea was meant to have milk and sugar in it, why wouldn't it be made that way in the first place?

The woman's expression turned from expectant to calculating, and then she nodded. "I think we'll do a bit of both. I think you'll like it better that way."

"Okay."

She added the milk, plopped two sugar cubes into the drink with the aid of a pair of silver tongs, and passed it over to him. He took the saucer carefully in his hand, watched as the cup and the liquid within it shook dangerously, and felt much relief when he finally placed both cup and saucer safely on the table.

"Have a cookie," said the woman.

Sebastian did as he was told and took a cookie and placed it on his saucer. He watched the woman add a drop of milk to her tea. She stirred it gently with a spoon and smiled at him. "Go on," she said, "give it a try."

Sebastian took a sip and found he rather did like tea with milk and sugar.

"Good?"

He nodded and she smiled. He took a bite of his cookie and then took another sip of his tea.

"Okay. Just so you understand what's going to happen," began the woman, "I'm going to call the police and have them come arrest you."

Sebastian sputtered and gagged on the tea. He felt a hotness inside his nose as the liquid found other ways to go than just down his throat. It caused a burning both in his mouth and behind his eyes. They watered a little, and finally, when he couldn't hold it in any longer, he erupted into a fit of coughing.

Eventually he was able to speak. "Arrest me?" he squeaked, and looked at the woman wide-eyed. "But why?"

"For trespassing," she replied matter-of-factly, leaning toward the tiered sweets tray. Her hand hovered over the little cakes, her fingers dancing in the air for a moment, as if they were the ones making the decision, not her. Eventually they chose a small pink cube. The woman took a bite and smiled approvingly at their choice.

"But I didn't trespass." His voice rose with every word. "I was asked in. I . . . I didn't even want to come in!" Sebastian could feel his cheeks heating up and his heart starting to race. He was flustered. He always got this way when things were unfair. There was no weapon against unreasonableness.

"That's all rather immaterial, I'm afraid," she said, taking another sip of tea. "Only society members are allowed in. It's a very clear rule."

"But I didn't know that. Why should I be punished for breaking a rule I didn't even know existed?"

"So if you murdered someone, but didn't know you weren't supposed to, you think you should not be punished for it?"

"That's totally different."

"How?"

Sebastian inhaled deeply, intent on explaining his reasoning, but as far as he could think, she was, unfortunately, correct. He had to take a different tactic. "Well, why should I believe you? How do I know it actually is a rule?"

The woman, who had brought her teacup toward her lips, froze for a moment and thought. Then she replaced the teacup on its saucer and abruptly stood, giving a sharp nod.

"Very well, come with me."

And with that Sebastian was following her again, sneaking his half-eaten cookie into his pocket as he rose. Down the rope ladder they went, across the freaky glass floor, onto the cobblestone path, and through the door. David Copperfield was at his side once again, a vigilant companion. Or, now that Sebastian thought about it, possibly more like a security guard. Maybe instead of a teeny helmet he needed a teeny headset: "The intruder is now making his way back down the stairs, over."

He walked back through the door-painting, and followed the woman onto the elevator. This time they only went down a few floors before it stopped and the woman exited. Sebastian followed her to the right and down the hall until she came to a door and turned to look at him.

"Now, this is going to be fun, but remember, we still have serious business to deal with."

". . . Okay?"

"No, really, this is going to be a blast." She sounded so serious that Sebastian seriously doubted the veracity of the statement.

The woman opened the door and Sebastian looked

around her to see what was beyond it. What he saw was surprising, yet surprisingly not totally out of place. It was the mouth of a slide, orange in color, and very much like the slide that was part of the jungle gym at his old school. He stepped in closer to get a better look, but the slide curved out of sight.

"I'll go first," the woman announced. She gently pushed Sebastian to the side and sat down at the mouth of the slide. Then, after a moment of stillness, she pushed herself into the orange tube and was gone, an ecstatic "Wheee!" drifting up from below.

Sebastian briefly considered turning around and going to the elevator and getting the heck out of there. But he had no idea if he could evade the woman by doing so. And besides . . . the slide did look like fun. He cautiously sat down, extending his legs out in front of him. He glanced at David Copperfield, who returned his look with an expression of "Oh, I'm not going down that thing," and then, after one final gaze down into the darkness, Sebastian pushed himself off the edge.

Whoosh, and he was sliding fast and furiously. It was almost scary, but really more like thrilling and all kinds of amazing. The slide curved and turned and twisted. Sebastian had absolutely no sense of where he was or which direction he was going. There was a moment when he sensed his hair sticking up on end and realized he was probably upside down. He didn't bother to contemplate the physics of the situation.

Suddenly he was thrown out of the tube and onto a pile of foam blocks. Actually more like a pit of foam blocks. He glanced around: the space was cavernous and the pit as large as a swimming pool. He looked up and saw the woman staring down at him at one end near an arched doorway, her hands on her hips, waiting expectantly.

"Well?" she asked.

Sebastian stared at her for a moment, and then understood. "Oh, a blast, a total blast."

"Told you so." She extended her hand to help Sebastian and he slowly made his way over to the side, pushing tediously through the never-ending foam blocks as he did, until finally he was able to grab it and, with her help, climb out of the pit. Once he was standing at her side, she gave that efficient nod of hers again. "But now it's time to get serious."

"Of course," he answered. She had, after all, warned him.

Sebastian followed her down a high-ceilinged hall, much brighter than the previous ones from upstairs and painted with pastel murals of some fantastical-looking place with centaurs and fairies. The woman stopped abruptly, turned to her right, opened a door that looked like part of the wall, and they entered a very small but extremely tall room, so tall that there was a skylight right at the top, which had to mean that the room was as tall as the building was.

Sebastian looked around in the dim light. The space was completely empty except for an old-fashioned wooden school desk with its chair attached. It even had a hole in the top of the desk where an inkpot would have gone once upon a time. Lying on the desk was a thick leather-bound book. The woman went to sit behind the desk and Sebastian followed, stopping in front of it. He looked down at the tome at its center, trying to make out what it said under the thick layer of dust that covered it.

On it was one word: *Rules*.

"I'd stand back if I were you," said the woman, and Sebastian stepped back obediently.

The woman took in a deep breath and then blew the dust off the cover of the book. It flew toward Sebastian in a cloud, and he backed himself right up against the wall. But it stopped short of him and, changing its mind, slowly spiraled upward, dancing in the light of the skylight.

The woman opened the book and after several moments of page turning exclaimed, "Aha!" She

looked at Sebastian with a victorious expression. "Come here, boy."

Once again he did precisely what she told him to do, and once again he marveled at how awfully compliant he was being. There was something about the woman that commanded respect. He hoped maybe someday he would have the same effect on people.

She turned the book around so that he could look at it, her finger still marking the spot, and Sebastian learned forward and squinted at the tiny print.

" 'Article 54, Section Q,' " the woman read. " 'Anyone caught trespassing, encroaching, or invading shall be handed over with haste and suspicion to the authorities.' "

Sebastian looked up and let out a frustrated huff. "But I was invited inside. I wasn't . . . encroaching," he said, his voice rising slightly.

The woman read on: " 'The definition of these terms is left to the discretion of the society members.' "

Oh. Well. Still didn't seem fair, though.

But rules are rules.

Except.

"Wait, what's that?" asked Sebastian.

"What's what?" asked the woman.

"That." Sebastian pointed to a tiny *15* beside the sentence.

"Hmm." The woman leaned closer to the book and so did Sebastian. They were so close that he could feel one of her gray curls tickling his forehead. Down at the bottom of the page, below a line, was a series of footnotes[7] written in an even smaller print. "Do you see 15?"

Sebastian squinted even more, not entirely certain there was any positive effect in doing so. He found the

---

[7] I just felt obligated to write a footnote for the word "footnotes." I actually don't have anything to say in particular.

tiny *15* and read the words beside it out loud slowly: " 'Unless of course an alternate suitable punishment can be agreed upon by the members, or if the members just don't feel like punishing anyone in the first place.' "

The woman sat up and leaned back in her seat. She tented her fingers together and brought them to her lips, contemplating what Sebastian had just read.

"Well, I mean, that's good, isn't it? We don't have to bother the police, who I'm sure have much more important things to deal with,[8] and it was all a misunderstanding, after all. I mean . . . it's obvious how harmless I am."

The woman said "Hmm" again and continued to tap her lips with her fingers.

"I'm not the sort of person who does wrong things. I'm really not," continued Sebastian, feeling the panic rise. "I wouldn't so much as move a piece of dust out of place without permission. I have no interest in upsetting the order of things. I don't like change, you see, and I am certain that however the members have decided to run this society must be good and I would never ever consider disrupting its day-to-day function-

---

[8] *Though as it turned out, the chief of police was at that moment watching his clock ticking ambivalently, and really wouldn't have minded the distraction.*

ing. Ever." He was beginning to sound a little desperate, even to himself, but it was all true. Of all the threats in the world, he was the least. He was the antithreat.

The woman stopped tapping and stared at him hard. "Say that again?"

"I'm not a rule-breaker. I never would have willingly broken the rules. I believe in order. In logic. In following the correct path." Oh, the correct path, the beautiful, happy, appropriate, correct path. The one that when you veered off it, you landed in stupid, thrilling society buildings with stupid, thrilling names.

With that now-familiar nod of hers, the woman stood up. "Well then. That settles it. You absolutely need to be punished."

Okay, that wasn't how he thought this encounter would end.

The woman came around to Sebastian's side of the desk and put a warm but firm hand on his shoulder. "Because quite frankly, I know no one in need of an attitude adjustment more than you."

➤ CHAPTER 4 ➤

In which we meet Evie.

Pathetic.

There was no better word for it.

Evie sat on the small ledge, staring out her small window, and imagined someone down in the street looking up, seeing her through the dusty pane of glass, her sad expression, her knees hugged to her chest. Would they have felt pity for the girl in the window? Even Evie knew it was all a bit too much, really. There was no way anyone could look that particularly miserable. *Maybe they're shooting a movie,* the person on the street might think. *But if so, where are the cameras?*

They couldn't see into the room, of course, but if they could, they would certainly have concluded that

this girl lived one of the most pathetic lives imaginable. Such a small gray little place. One desk. One chair. One bed. One set of drawers. And so few personal items that even if it had been possible to cheer up the space, she wouldn't have been able to.

But worse than her pathetic appearance and pathetic room was that she was, pathetically, at the moment, overwhelmingly full of self-pity.

"Buck up, Buttercup!" she said to herself, but as much as she pretended, it was her voice that she heard, not her mother's.

It had been two years. Two whole years.

Why did it still feel like this?

There was a knock on the door. Evie stared at it for a moment. No one at school ever knocked on her door.

"Yes?" she said.

The door opened, and Daisy's angular features materialized from behind it. "Oh, sorry," she said. "Wrong room." The girl smiled brightly and then closed the door.

Evie sat there seething with rage. Daisy knew this was her room; there was no mistaking it. She'd done that on purpose, just to rub it in that no one wanted to hang out with her. Just to make it explicitly clear. But Evie was well aware of that. She wasn't a fool. What she didn't know was why. Why she didn't fit in here? What was it that made the other girls avoid her? She had thought maybe they were jealous that she lived here year-round, that the state had brought her to the Wayward School and it was her home now. But who would be jealous of living at a school? Especially a school as uninteresting and uninspiring as Wayward?

Oh, it wasn't fair! She was so sick and tired of things being unfair! Without thinking, Evie grabbed the small cup of water on the bedside table and threw it against the door. That felt good! She stood up and tore the blanket off her small bed, and then grabbed the pencils on the desk and flung those. Then she pulled open her drawers and ripped the clothes out, tossing them everywhere. She grabbed her parents' picture and hurled it at the wall. . . .

Another knock on the door, but more like a heavy banging.

"What is going on in there?" demanded Mrs. Pomeranian, shoving the door open.

Evie stood still and wondered the same thing. She gazed, astonished, at the mess around her, felt the tears on her cheeks and stared wide-eyed at Mrs. Pomeranian, who glowered back at her down her long pointy nose.

"I'm . . . sorry. . . ."

"This is unacceptable!" Mrs. Pomeranian walked slowly into the room, shaking her head at the destruction. Her voice was high and plummy and full of disdain. Evie knew it well; she'd never heard anything else from Mrs. Pomeranian. At least, not when her house mistress spoke with her in particular. "When we agreed to take you on as your full-time guardians, we laid out very strict rules of behavior. We were guaranteed that you would abide by them. But you, little Miss Evie, have done nothing to integrate yourself into our community here. You make no friends. You sulk in your room."

But it wasn't as if she hadn't tried. "I'm sorry," Evie said quietly.

"And you were chosen by the Andersons to be their guest at their home once a week. For two years in a row now. Something quite unusual." She sniffed the air after saying that, as if the unusualness of the situation came with a particularly bad smell. "You keep up your pouting and they might just revoke the privilege."

Evie scoffed inwardly. She wouldn't mind at all if they took back the invitation. Her weekly Wednesday dinner at the Andersons' was one of the most boring experiences that could be experienced. It couldn't even really be called an "experience." It just simply *was*.

No, she chastised herself instantly. It was the one time a week she got to escape this prison. She shouldn't be so ungrateful.

Mrs. Pomeranian approached and squinted down at her.

"Why can't you just be happy, Evie?"

"I want to," Evie replied, forcing the tears to stay buried and causing her throat to constrict so much she thought she might choke.

Mrs. Pomeranian looked at the bed, gave it a pat, and sat down on the edge.

"I'm not trying to be mean to you," she said, her

expression softening a bit so that the deep creases across her forehead were slightly shallower. "I know you've gone through a lot. But this is your life, Evie. And the only thing you can do is accept it."

Evie tried to swallow, but it was impossible. Why couldn't Mrs. Pomeranian just leave her alone? "I . . . can't do that."

"Well, then," said Mrs. Pomeranian, standing, "you're never going to be happy."

Evie didn't know what to say to that. What a thought. And it didn't make any sense. After all, if she accepted that she was totally and completely alone in the world—no family, no one who loved her—then she would be very sad indeed. But if she didn't accept that, then she would also be sad? No, no, that couldn't be true.

"The moment you understand that this is it is the moment you can start living your life." Mrs. Pomeranian looked around the room and shook her head. "Now clean up this mess."

Evie nodded as Mrs. Pomeranian swept out of the room, closing the door behind her. A peal of giggles could be heard out in the hall, and Evie was pretty sure Daisy and her friends had been listening to their conversation. But she wasn't angry anymore. She was just . . . defeated.

One by one, she started picking up the pieces of her room. She bent over and picked up the framed picture of her parents. There was a crack across the glass now, and Evie felt a pang in her gut.

"I'm sorry," she said, touching the glass with her finger. She placed the picture gingerly on the small table by her bed and sat down and stared at it. It was a picture from before Evie was born, one she had always kept by her bed at home, which she'd stolen out of the family album because she loved it so much. Her parents were having a picnic on the side of a mountain, with a winding river far below them and snowcapped peaks in the distance. They looked so happy and free. On an adventure. Like the adventures they used to go on, all three of them, as a family. Hiking, or skiing, or taking a boat far out to sea.

"Life's an adventure," her mom used to say.

"No it's not," Evie said aloud now. "It's four gray walls and a dusty window."

Then she rolled her eyes and sighed, and flopped herself down on her mattress, still staring at the photograph.

Yup.

Pathetic.

CHAPTER 5

In which we learn about Sebastian's punishment.

Sebastian's punishment was not going to jail or even paying a fine. It turned out that the woman had something else in mind for him. He was to come to society headquarters every day after school and help keep the place in order. Or out of order, depending on what was needed at the time. He was given a special key and instructed that no visitors were allowed inside unless they were allowed inside. He was to sweep and dust and vacuum, reshelve books, or pull books off the shelf and throw them on the floor. He was to change David Copperfield's litter box and feed Hubert's pig in a teeny hat, his gerbils, his rats, and his budgies. Additionally he was assigned the task of doing anything else that was required. He was what the woman called a jack-of-all-trades. Sebastian considered it more like a personal servant . . . but whatever.

The fact was that it hardly felt like a punishment. And his parents approved of it, as they believed it would teach him some new skills. And so Sebastian came to know the wondrous, strange, sometimes itchy Explorers Society.

He also came to know the woman's name: Myrtle Algens. She was the current president of The Explorers Society. Myrtle had become a member of the society at the young age of nineteen after she had accompanied her father and mother on an expedition to the North Pole to ascertain, in no uncertain terms, that there were no penguins there. "It had always seemed to my father that there ought to be penguins there. It was just as cold and brutal as the South Pole. Why wouldn't they want to live there, too? Of course, there were no penguins there. Not one. But I do believe to his dying day he really thought they were there. Somewhere." After that she had returned to the North Pole half a dozen times, leading a couple of expeditions herself. "The expeditions were a little dull. People just want to see if they can do it, can handle the cold, the bleak whiteness. And, as it turns out, they always can. It doesn't hurt that they have expensive snowsuits and state-of-the-art winter camping gear." She had been given the nickname of

Ice Queen at the society, but a kind of warmth always glowed from beneath her pragmatic shell. Sebastian determined quite quickly that he liked her a lot.

Now, Sebastian had always known he'd eventually have to get a job. That was an inevitability of growing up. It was drilled home hard at school, with essay assignments at least once a year about plans for the future. He had just never thought that he would have a job quite so soon, and that it would involve such a random collection of tasks. But here he was dusting every inch of The Explorers Society, doing cartwheels, washing windows, reciting Shakespeare's thirty-third sonnet. All the while being followed and kept close tabs on by a pig in a teeny hat.

And he was enjoying every moment of it.

It wasn't the tasks themselves (mind you, he was proud that he had finally conquered the vacuum). It was where he was. It was the people he was meeting. The members.

Like Belinda Carey, her hair multicolored like a tie-dyed shirt, who spent her days exploring the various sewer systems of cities in Europe and who was always the first person to call on if the toilet broke in the building. Or Tom Argall, who liked to immerse himself in the complex hierarchical world of leaves, sitting at the tops of trees for months until they adapted to him and made him part of the canopy. There was Lady Trill, who had a fondness for desert islands, and once survived an entire year with only a paperclip and a snow globe. And there was August C. Bourré, who believed the greatest adventures one could have were in one's own backyard. He was infamous for having the largest number of arrests for trespassing in the backyards and gardens of various families around the world.

Of course there were more of them, and those who weren't presently in the city and able to use the society headquarters were talked about so much that it seemed as if they were there.

And it wasn't just the stories that were thrilling, it was the society headquarters itself.

Which room was his favorite? Could he even choose? The obvious one would have to be the library, which was also a kind of enclosed central courtyard. The space rose the height of the entire building, with books shelved floor to ceiling. At each floor of the building there ran a balcony around all sides that allowed access to books and also various rooms beyond. The tree grew there, tall and thick, its roots somewhere in the basement and its trunk rising up and up until it burst through the ceiling and continued up with its tree teahouse. Somehow, some clever soul had managed to fashion steps that wrapped around and through its trunk, allowing you access to all the levels of the room.

The library collection was vast. Each level had its own theme, and of course, Sebastian was most drawn to level four: the Human and Worldly and Not-So-Worldly Biology section. Not only did it have books on every species on the planet, and some books on species Sebastian was skeptical truly existed, it also had the most spectacular creature in the entire Explorers Society. Stretching the breadth of the north section of the library was a large skeleton of an Elasmosaurus, the long-necked carnivorous swimming dinosaur from the Late Cretaceous period that kind of looked like a brontosaurus from the torso up, but then it had fins instead of legs, and long sharp teeth. The skeleton was lit by blue and green lights for a fantastic effect that made it easy for Sebastian to picture it swimming through deep ancient seas.

There was also a room off the east side of level four that was filled with specimen jars containing all kinds of bugs and insects. But the most fascinating and probably freakiest part was the large room behind a hidden door made to look just like one of the bookshelves. You pulled on the book entitled *Human Kinesiology* and a room filled with actual human bodies was revealed. These bodies were stripped of skin, highlighting all the various muscles and tendons, and they were posed as if in action, revealing how the inner workings of the body would respond in different activities. One body was doing yoga, another was preparing to jump, another was baking a cake. All the bodies, Sebastian had learned, had been donated to the society, gifted by their owners in their wills (including the great Shakespearean actor Jonathan Llyr, sitting and holding his own head in the classic Hamlet pose).

Of course . . . there was also level five, the engineering level, and he couldn't help but enjoy that one as well, considering everything his sister had told him about the subject. And there was a replica of the Wright brothers' plane taking up much of the west side of the room, which was an extraordinary thing to see every day.

There was also the geology level with all its sparkling rocks and all its dull rocks, which turned out to be far more interesting in some ways than the sparkling ones.

There was the chemistry level . . .

There were lots of amazing levels.

So the library was the obvious first choice. But the library wasn't everything.

"There's more?" Sebastian had asked, his mouth

still open wide from the awe he'd experienced upon first entering the library.

"Always assume there's something more, Sebastian. That's a good life lesson," Myrtle replied in that matter-of-fact way of hers.

He had been shown the locker room where the explorers kept their personal belongings: "Make sure all the boots point toward Mount Kilimanjaro," Myrtle had instructed.

He had seen the kitchens, where international chef-adventurer Tobias Wallace spent most of his time, experimenting with varied and unusual flavors. "This is from my latest expedition through the sulfur caves of Morocco," he said, pointing to a small fishbowl. Sebastian looked more closely and saw what seemed to be puffs of smoke moving about. "Gaseous carp. They smell and taste like rotten eggs. They're fantastic. Would you like to try?" Tobias held up a small flaky pastry and Sebastian shook his head.

"Uh, I just ate. Next time?"

"Let me put some in Tupperware for you. You can take them home to your parents."

"Oh. Thanks."

There was also the room piled high with empty Tupperware containers. "Just dump the contents into the compost hole there," Myrtle had directed. Sebastian did and placed the empty container on top of a teetering pile. "We return all the containers at the end of the month. And the composting does wonders for the tree."

Then there was the greenhouse, an addition to the rear of the building, all in glass framed by delicate Art Nouveau ironwork. It peaked in a Gothic arch, and swirls of wrought-iron vines and leaves grew up the supports. Warm and muggy, it was tended to by a husband and wife pair, the Dryers. Flora from all over the world could be found there: tall, slender trees with wide, flat green and orange leaves; small purple flowers that sent their pollen flying in bursts of purple and pink every fifty-nine minutes. Roses and daffodils, sunflowers and cacti. And it seemed almost every explorer had their own plot devoted to their own particular interests—transplanted items rescued from extinction, or weeds extracted from an overgrowth for further investigation.

Possibly the room that confused Sebastian the most was the leather chair room. It wasn't that the room itself was confusing; it was pretty straightforward, actually. It was a room with a lot of leather chairs. Some were low and boxlike; others were tall wingbacks. Some were nothing more than stools with leather tops.

They were all placed in groupings around low coffee tables in alcoves. Here members of the society would meet to relax, have a compelling conversation, or nap, isolated on their own. The latter really applied only to Henry McGuin, a small bald man who seemed always to be sleeping in the northeast corner, arms folded across his chest, his head leaning into the right seam of his chair. Games of various kinds sat on tables of various kinds, and cards were a particular favorite of the members, who sat playing with them for hours, laughing but also getting fiercely furious at times.

This room confused Sebastian so much not because of what was in it, but because of how it made him feel. Which was mostly out of place. As if he was still trespassing even though he wasn't anymore. As if he shouldn't be there, didn't fit in or belong. It wasn't just that he was a kid and everyone else was a grown-up. No, Sebastian had always been able to get along quite well with grown-ups. It was that he wasn't an explorer. He couldn't share stories, couldn't share laughs. All he could do was wipe away the odd watermark and clear up crumbs with the handheld vacuum and dust around the objects in the large glass case between windows labeled with such interesting titles as "Dragonlace Vase, 33 BC" and "Flaming Mosquito Bicuspid, 1969" and "Gold Orb, date unknown."

But more than just a weird feeling, there was a sense of longing. A sense that not fitting in mattered to him in a way that not fitting in had never mattered. He had never felt a need to be popular at school, to find that social grouping that would finally give him a sense of belonging. He had never thought he didn't belong in the first place. Maybe it was because he had always perfectly belonged with his family. Maybe it was because belonging didn't really affect his future career options.

Here, though, at The Explorers Society . . . Here. Here he hated that he didn't really belong. That he was here because, without knowing it, he'd done something wrong. He hadn't earned the right to be here. He hadn't even known what here was until just a couple of days ago. The leather chair room was the room where the members gathered to talk about their adventures old and upcoming, the room most populated by members at any given moment, and it was the room where Sebastian felt most out of place, surrounded by so many amazing people who *had* earned the right to be in the society.

So it was with great trepidation that he pushed open the door to the leather chair room and went in. There was thankfully only one small group toward the back by the windows. In short order, Sebastian had pushed the chairs back into place, mopped up three spilled drinks, and dusted off the tables and window-sills. Maybe tomorrow he should wash the windows?

He finally approached the group in the back. One gentleman Sebastian didn't recognize gave him a small nod, and Sebastian quickly grabbed a couple of empty glasses and cleared a few crumpled napkins. There was, of course, a waitstaff who could do that as well, but he really wanted to impress the members. Stand out. Go beyond the call of duty.

For some reason.

"The Ice Queen cometh," said Lady Trill with a smile, and Sebastian instinctively looked over his shoulder. Sure enough, Myrtle was making her way toward the group. She sat down in a low-slung chair and reclined, releasing a contented sigh. Then she looked at Sebastian.

"Good! Sebastian, have a seat. We need to talk."

He didn't need to be ordered twice, not by anyone usually, and certainly not by Myrtle. Sebastian pulled up a small stool and sat facing the group.

"Do you know everyone here?" she asked.

Sebastian nodded. "Almost everyone. Lady Trill, Edmund Banks, the Hopper. I don't know that gentle-man." He gestured toward the man sitting to her left.

"I'm Llewellyn Tracy," replied the man in a

melodious voice. He smiled politely and stroked his neatly trimmed black beard.

"Nice to meet you."

"Sebastian, I need to ask you something, and you have to be honest with me," said Myrtle, leaning forward and looking at him hard.

"I always am." He sat a little straighter in his chair, ready to answer any question she should ask in the most efficient and direct way possible.

"Yes, I know, so unfortunate. What exactly have you been getting up to in the time since you started working here?"

Was it a trick question? Sebastian couldn't tell. He hadn't found Myrtle to be anything other than extraordinarily straightforward. And yet, wasn't the answer kind of obvious? "Well, I mean, the stuff you told me to do," he answered hesitantly. "Cleaning."

Myrtle sighed hard and leaned back in her seat. She gave Lady Trill a look, and the long-haired brunette shook her head.

"Did I say something wrong?" He slouched ever so slightly, not happy with the idea that he might have displeased her.

"If I may," said Llewellyn Tracy, "I'm afraid the issue is that you've done something right. And not just *something,* but everything." It sounded as if it ought to be a compliment, but his singsongy voice was in a minor key.

"I . . ." Sebastian had nothing. "I don't get it."

"Do you know why the society agreed to let your punishment be to help out instead of calling the police or wiping your mind of the memories of your visit here?" asked the Hopper, a small man in plaid sitting on the edge of his chair, feet dangling above the floor.

"Wait—you can do that?"

"No, of course not. No such technology exists. Besides, there are the moral implications. The point was that we had other options, both real and imaginary, and yet we agreed to this one. Why do you think that is?"

The answer was obvious. Or maybe it wasn't. Sebastian was feeling less sure of himself by the moment. "Because you needed the extra help?" he asked tentatively.

Myrtle leaned toward him once again and took his hand in hers. It was soft and warm, as if she were wearing a well-worn leather glove. "Because *you* needed the extra help."

"With what?"

"With pushing the boundaries, with breaking the rules, with getting yourself into trouble."

"Why on earth would I want to do any of those

things?" Just thinking about it made his stomach tighten, and it felt as if something heavy were suddenly sitting on his chest.

"Sebastian, do you know how penicillin was discovered?"

"Uh . . . I think it was by accident," replied Sebastian.

"Yes," said Myrtle. "Because the man who discovered it, Mr. Fleming, had been remiss in cleaning his petri dishes and mold had grown. If he had been like you with your mop and bucket, imagine what a different world this would be."

Now, this was hardly fair, and Sebastian was starting to get sincerely angry. His punishment was that he was supposed to help out at the headquarters, and cleaning it had been a big part of that. They had told him to mop the floors. Shown him where the bucket was kept. It wasn't as if he had appeared on their stoop just begging the members to clean up after them or anything.

"So now you don't want me to clean? Fine, I'm happy not to clean. Should I just sit here, then?"

"Oh my, he's gone all petulant," said the Hopper in what could only be described as a condescending tone.

"At least he's talking back a little," replied Llewellyn Tracy.

"Sebastian." Myrtle ignored the others, her gaze pinned on Sebastian as if she was studying him carefully. "Some time in the next week I want you to do something inappropriate, okay?"

Sebastian inwardly rolled his eyes and outwardly frowned. "Sure, fine, whatever." It seemed so silly, so stupid. And anyway, was it really inappropriate if he did what was asked of him? And why did any of it matter? He lived a perfectly good life. A perfectly appropriate life.

But he still had that spark of determination to prove himself to them for some reason, and so Sebastian began his campaign over the next several days, resolved that somehow he would manage to do something "inappropriate." He left his water glass on the wooden table in the hallway instead of on a coaster. Well, he tried to, at any rate, but it just didn't feel right punishing a vintage Louis XVI table when he was the one in trouble, so he quickly removed it a moment later. He ignored his summons to the leather chair room . . . for a full five minutes. He even showed up late one day for work, sitting outside playing with his key to the headquarters for twenty minutes until he finally came inside. No one remotely noticed.

It all seemed so pointless, and as the week wore on, Sebastian wondered if maybe he could just lie. Lying, after all, was inappropriate, and maybe he could say he'd done something truly terrible when no one was watching. People rarely watched him.

Except when they did.

It was when he decided to tackle the archives that Sebastian finally found his moment of inappropriateness. And much like mold growing in an unwashed petri dish, this moment of inappropriateness grew from something slightly unpleasant into something that would change the course of a person's life: Sebastian's.

Dramatic music plays now.

Or . . . not.

(Okay, who's in charge of the dramatic music, because I was told it was going to play now and it hasn't and this is seriously unacceptable.)

CHAPTER 6

In which we discover
A PLAIN
WOODEN BOX!!!!

The archives were Sebastian's least favorite part of the society headquarters. It wasn't that what they contained wasn't interesting. In fact, there were some fascinating personal histories filed under Q that he had started to read. It was just that the place was impossible to keep clean. No matter how hard he dusted, there was always a layer of grime that wouldn't go away. Even when he tried with soap and water and really scrubbed, the tops of the filing cabinets, the tables, the floors, all of it stayed stained and the dust would find its way back again. Like an irritating game of hide-and-seek. The particles waited for him to leave the room, and then each piece of dust would dutifully float back into place.

Possibly part of the reason for this was that the archives were little more than a hollowed-out cave in the ground. The roots of the great tree pushed through the ceiling above him and twisted their way down the walls. The floor was covered in a kind of stone, but even so the earth peeked through, and could never be fully swept away.

Aside from the cleanliness factor, the room was also gloomy, lit by a single bulb, a bland pale light that hardly escaped its own glass encasing. It would make Sebastian's eyes grow heavy. And time would seem meaningless and work would happen in slow motion. Sometimes even appearing to run backward.

This was why Sebastian didn't actually mind the company of the pig in the teeny hat, despite the fact that it always seemed like the pig was judging him a little bit. Sebastian would talk to the pig to keep himself awake and focused. And on occasion he could swear that it did appear as though the pig could understand him.

"See! This is what I mean! I just cleaned that spot five minutes ago and it's filthy again!" Sebastian said, and the pig gave a little snort back in what Sebastian hoped was solidarity.

Sebastian sighed hard. "Pass me the scrub brush?" he asked, knowing full well the pig would have no idea what he was asking for. But the pig turned and looked, stood up, and wandered over to the scrub brush. Sebastian watched in amazement as the pig picked it up and came trotting over to him. "Uh, thanks . . . ," said Sebastian, reaching out to take the brush from the pig's mouth.

But the pig didn't stop. Instead it trotted past Sebastian to the other side of the room and then placed the brush on the floor. Sebastian sighed and walked over to pick it up. Just as the pig grabbed it in its mouth again and trotted away. "Oh," said Sebastian, not remotely amused, "you're playing keep-away. Not cool, pig."

Sure enough, as Sebastian walked over again to grab the brush, the pig darted past him. And again. And again. In short order Sebastian was chasing the pig around the room and was pretty certain anyone watching would have found the situation the height of absurdity. Finally he had the pig cornered and lunged at it. The pig rushed at Sebastian, aiming to run between his legs but instead tripping him up, causing him to fall hard on his back. The pig slid across the floor and rammed into an old wooden filing cabinet, causing its hat to topple off its head and sending a mountain of papers flying off the top of the cabinet and down behind it.

Sebastian watched all this happen from his upside-down perspective and sighed. "Thanks for that, pig," he said, pushing himself upright and rubbing the back of his head.

He stood up and brushed the dust off his trousers, then went over to the cabinet. He looked down at the pig, who looked up at him complacently. He picked up the hat and placed it back on its head. Then he turned and faced the filing cabinet. Sebastian put his hands on his hips and appraised it for a moment. And then he rolled up his sleeves, grabbed the cabinet with both hands, and pulled.

And pulled.

And pulled.

The pig snorted.

Finally the cabinet started to slide out from against the wall and Sebastian got down on his knees to grab at the fallen folders behind it.

He was hardly shocked to discover that behind it there were dust bunnies so huge one could have possibly called them dust hippos. But what did surprise him was that on the reverse of the very dull, nondescript filing cabinet was a door.

It was small, no higher than his knee. And it looked very much like a front door to a house. Quite fancy, really. So what could Sebastian do but open it?

Now, reader, there are generally surprises on the other sides of mysterious doors found hidden in cave-like archives—secret passageways, portals to other worlds, forgotten rooms—but what Sebastian found was far more exciting. You see, Sebastian found a box.

A very plain, and very wooden, and very average-sized box.

I know. Exciting, right?

Sebastian removed the box and looked at it. It was simple—an average, everyday wooden box—and it bore one marking. A strange, shallow carving on its top. It looked like this:

"This could be inappropriate," Sebastian said to the pig. The pig sniffed the box and snorted. Sebastian took that as a positive sign and smiled. He had a good feeling that he could finally be completing his illicit assignment.

It was the end of his shift by this point, so Sebastian sneaked the box upstairs and slipped it quickly into his knapsack. He walked apace, not able to make eye contact with anyone and only nodding in return to the goodbyes the few members made as he returned to the first floor. Then he darted out the main door and practically ran home.

What a weight off his shoulders it was, knowing he had finally done what Myrtle had asked him to do. What a weight *on* his shoulders it was, carrying the darn box home.

Sebastian kept his pace up straight through his own front door. He pulled it closed behind him, zipped through the hallway, and rushed up the stairs past his mother, who shook her head, and he threw open his bedroom door and locked it behind him. It was the first time in his life that he had used the lock on his door, and if he hadn't been so excited about the box, he might have thought about what it meant that he wanted to prevent his parents from coming in and seeing what he was up to. Instead of thinking that, however, he swept aside all his maps strewn about on the floor from yesterday, when he'd been comparing the lengths of rivers, and pulled the box from his knapsack.

Sebastian placed the box in the middle of the floor and sat cross-legged in front of it. And stared at it. Aside from the strange symbol on the top, there were no other markings, as far as he could see. There was no clasp or lock either, but there must be a way in. He just needed to figure it out.

He picked up the box and had a very close look at it. He noticed that the front and back sides appeared to be made of three panels: two large ones and one narrow one in the middle. He pushed into the narrow middle panel. Nothing happened. Then he tried to slide it toward the front. And it moved. But only maybe a quarter of an inch.

He did the same action on the other side and wondered what exactly was the advantage to a box opening only a quarter of an inch like that. As he turned the box over in his hands, the square panel on the far end of the box slid downward. A quarter of an inch. But now this quarter of an inch was becoming meaningful.

Following the pattern, Sebastian attempted to move the long top piece with the symbol on it, and sure enough, with the square side now a half-inch lower, the top of the box could be slid open . . . a quarter of an inch.

The pride he felt in having made this accomplishment was quickly replaced with frustration when he couldn't figure out exactly how to get any further. He tried closing all the sides up again and starting from scratch. Still the box only opened a quarter of an inch. His temperature was rising; his cheeks were flushed with anger. There had to be a reasonable solution. He stared up close at the box, and as he slid each panel carefully back into place, he tried to sneak a peek to see how the darn thing worked. But the box wasn't giving up its secrets.

"Sebastian!" his mother yelled from downstairs. "Dinnertime!" He let out a breath he hadn't realized he was holding, put the box on his bed, and left his room to join his parents.

He sat down hoping dinner would pass relatively quickly. He wasn't feeling particularly hungry, and he pushed his food around his plate aimlessly.

"I don't understand," said his mother with a worried expression on her face, "I thought brussels sprouts were your favorite."

Shoot. He didn't want them to get suspicious that something was wrong. "Oh, they are. They are," he said quickly, and shoveled some into his mouth. He tried to chew and smile at the same time, which just made his mother's eyebrows furrow more. But she didn't say anything else.

Finally, after another agonizing fifteen minutes, he was allowed to leave the table. He went straight back up to his room and picked up the box, feeling pretty sorry for himself.

He absently started pushing the sliding pieces of the box in and out again, in and out. What was the solution? Was he not smart enough to solve it? In and out. In and out. That was a scary thought, though he supposed there was always something more to learn. Even for him.

In and out.

And suddenly the other square side panel moved. Sebastian froze, frightened that the slightest motion might undo his accident. For the first time since Myrtle's assignment he understood the value of not doing something by the book. He realized he had mistakenly slid the narrow side pieces back to their original positions first, not last, when he had been reversing all the sliding pieces. This accident had resulted in the new square panel moving. Then he tried sliding the narrow pieces out again, and they moved even farther! A whole half inch! Then! Then the original square piece moved a half inch and then the top piece . . . slid off completely.

Sebastian hadn't expected anything to slide off, so when it did, it practically flew across the room. He stared into the box at the contents. It was full of carefully placed old photographs and newspaper articles. Delicately, Sebastian pulled each piece out and examined it.

There was a large black-and-white photograph of five people sitting in front of a giant map. A very familiar giant map. Oh! Sebastian knew exactly what map it was. It was the map on the wall in the giant map room at the society headquarters! He examined the image more closely, going down the line of people. They all looked very serious, and a little smug. No, not smug, just . . . proud.

Sebastian pulled out a newspaper article. An attractive woman with a short bob, wearing a very crisp-looking khaki jacket and trousers, was smiling at the camera with her arm carefully draped over the body of a large, squat, furry creature that seemed part tiger, part bear. It was looking at her fondly. The caption read "The Filipendulous Five Discover the Banded Bearcat."

Another article and another picture. A somber-looking man, head shaved, arms folded across his chest standing knee-deep in a jungle river. "Benedict Barnes, now of the Filipendulous Five, began his career as a cartographer but discovered a passion for photography after capturing the moment Joyce Styles became the first person to scale Mount Impossible by arriving ahead of her to set up the camera."

And yet another. A man with dark hair and a trimmed beard, wearing sunglasses and a three-piece suit. He was pointing into the distance. "Alistair Drake Chooses the Correct Path."

And still more articles and pictures. Some official-looking, some candid. Laughter at a birthday party. The clinking of glasses at a fancy dinner. But the best pictures weren't of people at all. The best pictures were of castles on top of mountains, and rushing rivers over waterfalls, cities with towers reflecting a blinding sun, remote cottages dwarfed by redwoods. There was a tightrope across a gorge, a statue of a man with a bird head as tall as a skyscraper. There were animals and vistas and people. Lots of people of different sizes, shapes, and colors.

Cars, and trains, and planes, and a hot-air balloon.

And a submarine. At least, that was what it looked like to Sebastian. Its top poked out of the water, gleaming wet. Where had it been? Where was it going?

Whoever the Filipendulous Five were, they led one

heck of an impressive life. They also seemed to be rather fond of each other, and Sebastian felt twinges of both excitement and jealousy as he read of their exploits and examined each photograph carefully. What an amazing group of people.

He glanced over at the lid of the box across the room and stared at it for a good long while. Then he looked back at the pictures of all the places and people and things. . . .

Explorers.

They were quite obviously a group of explorers. It made perfect sense. Such a box was what you'd expect to find in a headquarters for explorers. It was hardly out of place. So why exactly had the box been stowed out of the way in the archives like that? Surely it belonged on a shelf like any of the other historical documents kept there, and not hidden away, stashed behind some secret door. And why had he never heard their names before? Or at least the name of their team? Why did none of these pictures grace the walls of the society like the many others of their fellow members?

Sebastian picked up the large group photo and stared at it. Such confident, assured faces. Who exactly *were* the Filipendulous Five? And what did they have to hide?

Aside from plain wooden boxes, of course.

CHAPTER 7

In which we attend a different kind of dinner party.

Awkward dinner parties were Evie's least favorite kind of parties. They came in well below themed parties, and absolutely below political parties. They made her retinas ache from that special blend of discomfort and boredom. Unfortunately, though they were her least favorite kind, Evie had been to many of these parties. In fact, she could safely say that she had attended far more awkward dinner parties than any other kind of party in her short life. Far more than birthday parties, that was certain.

Now that she thought about it, maybe she hated birthday parties more. No one ever invited her to those, so she could really only count the eleven she had had for herself. And then there was the part about how her parents, the people responsible for bringing her into the world and creating that day for her, had left it two years ago. Yes, possibly birthday parties were worse than awkward dinner parties. But not by much.

In Evie's world, awkward dinner parties always happened at the same place. At the same time. With the same people. They happened once a week, and had been happening that way ever since she had been brought to the Wayward School. For some reason, two weeks into her new life as a person with no connections, no family, no anything, the Andersons had taken a kind of pity on her and had invited her to dinner at their modest but comfortable home just up the street. It had been an awfully sweet gesture, and Evie did appreciate their generosity. But . . . they were a really boring couple. Not particularly good at small talk, and only capable of asking Evie what was new in school that particular week. Though they did seem sincerely interested in her answers.

She'd now been attending their weekly dinners for almost two years. And they never got any less awkward. They always happened the same way, with the same kind of food. How many times had she sat staring at the inoffensive beige main course and then at the inoffensive beige dessert that replaced it? Evie never really knew what to say to the Andersons, who were very beige in their own way. Both were pale and lanky, with ash-blond hair cut short in the same efficient style. Their clothes were usually loose-fitting argyle sweaters and khaki slacks. She didn't ask them questions, because she'd found out quickly that they didn't like talking about themselves. Even when she'd asked why they liked the bland kind of food they did, Mrs. Anderson had just replied, "Oh, we've had enough excitement to last a lifetime."

What that excitement might have been, neither Mrs. nor Mr. Anderson ever expanded on. So theirs was always a conversation of fits and starts, and one where the loud grandfather clock out in the hall seemed to have the most to say.

But nothing could have prepared Evie for the awkwardness of this present Anderson dinner party. For while it was one thing to sit staring at beige food, listening to the archaic ticking of the clock in the hall and waiting for dinner to finish, it was quite another to sit staring at a large old-fashioned-looking gun and two daggers on the plate across from her. It was also quite another to stare at the large man dressed in a black leather jacket and reflective aviator sunglasses sitting directly opposite.

But even more awkward than all that was the fact that Evie could make no attempt at small talk with the man, for it did appear that his jaw was wired shut. It was quite possibly the most disturbing thing she had ever seen. It clearly hadn't been a quality surgeon who'd done the job. Bits of rusty metal wire poked through from between his lips, and one sharp piece protruded right through the flesh of his cheek. And when the man grimaced, which he had done only once when he'd first seen Evie, he revealed a mess of rusty wires crisscrossing his top and bottom teeth, connecting them to each other, making it impossible for him to open his mouth. And it was very difficult for her not to stare, even though she knew it was a terribly rude thing to do.

The Andersons sat at either end of the table, as they always did, and Evie observed that their eating had taken on a slower pace than usual and that their hands shook more than was typical. She didn't blame them. Her own heart was pumping fast and she had no appetite whatsoever. Probably a good thing, really. She had the distinct impression, though the man hadn't said a word (how could he have?), that something bad was going to happen once dinner was over.

The man had appeared at the door during the cocktail hour. The Andersons always hosted a cocktail hour before dinner. To prolong the dullness of the evening, Evie supposed. Though she did like the sparkling apple cider she was always given. The bell had rung and Mrs. Anderson had gone off to answer the door. Evie and Mr. Anderson were left to stare at each other mildly, only to be interrupted by the sound of a glass shattering against the marble tile of the hallway floor.

For the first time since she'd known them, Evie saw real emotion cross Mr. Anderson's face, and he was up out of his seat and at his wife's side so quickly that Evie hadn't had a moment to process the action. She sat alone in the living room, wondering whether she should get up and join them at the door.

A few seconds later both the Andersons were escorted by the man back into the living room and over to the couch. Evie heard Mr. Anderson say, "It's not here." There was a quaver to his voice as he said it, and it had frightened Evie to hear him so scared. It was when the Andersons and the man had walked past Evie that she had noticed the large old-fashioned-looking gun pressed into the small of Mrs. Anderson's back, and the firm grip the man had on Mrs. Anderson's wrist. Evie stared in shock, and in that shock found that she couldn't do anything but . . . sit there.

Soon all four of them were sitting in total silence until the cocktail hour passed, and then, acting as if there was nothing amiss, they moved to the dining room table. This was when the man placed his gun on the extra place setting and removed two daggers from somewhere around his middle, in order, Evie assumed, to make it more comfortable for him to sit.

Dessert happened. And Evie glanced up at Mrs. Anderson, who placed a bowl of banana pudding in front of her and then sat down and stared at her own with a look of intense concentration. Her breathing was shallow but measured. Evie could hear it even from where she sat. She looked over at Mr. Anderson, who was staring at his wife with an expression of deep remorse. He was so tense, his neck muscles twitched.

What on earth was going on?

Having been too scared to speak up since it had all begun, Evie suddenly felt very protective of the Andersons. Sure, they were as dull as dishwater, or possibly even duller—dishwater at least had some bubbles to play with—but they had been kind to her for really no reason, and did give her a nice escape from the monotony that was the Wayward School. She liked them and she didn't like to see them scared like this, so Evie decided she had to say something to the man, no matter how frightened she felt.

"Uh . . . see here . . . sir . . . I don't . . ."

"Promise you won't hurt the girl," said Mrs. Anderson at the same time, and Evie stopped short.

The man gave Mrs. Anderson a look.

"She's an orphan. She goes to the state school down the street. Every year we find a child to support who needs it. She isn't . . . *important.*"

Despite the unfortunate circumstances, for the first time Evie had a better understanding of her situation with the Andersons and was, frankly, offended. Her cheeks burned and she looked down at her pudding bowl. It kind of sucked to be reminded how little she mattered to anyone in the world. She knew deep down there were greater issues at stake at the moment, but she couldn't help her feelings. Feelings just feel. It's what they do.

The man didn't respond.

"Trudy dear, would you pass the salt?" asked Mr. Anderson. Mrs. Anderson looked up from her pudding and then, after a moment, silently picked up the saltshaker. She leaned across the table, extending her hand holding the salt, and her husband did the same to receive it. The moment of saltshaker passing was reflected in the man's sunglasses.

Mr. Anderson shook some salt onto his pudding and placed the shaker to the side, not quite letting go of it, as if it were a security blanket of some kind.

"Please," said Mrs. Anderson, after the salt passing had been completed, "just let the child go."

Evie looked at Mrs. Anderson, then at the man. The

man looked at Mrs. Anderson, then at Evie. She saw reflected in his glasses what she assumed he saw, her face, small and pale, framed by wisps of light brown curls, a figure sitting low at the table, too old to require a booster seat but not quite at a comfortable height. She looked stupidly young, much younger than she felt. Maybe it would work in her favor. Then again, if it did, and the man let her go, she didn't feel right just leaving the Andersons there alone. There must be something she could do.

The man slowly shook his head side to side. An ominous "No." Evie's heart sank, as did her noble intentions. Maybe she could make a run for it. Though, she reasoned, if that were an option, surely the Andersons would have already tried such a thing. There was something more going on here, she realized just then. This man was no random thief in the night.

She glanced at Mr. Anderson, who just sat there, eating his salted pudding. He kept his head bowed. Meek. She felt sorry for him. She felt sorry for all of them. Would they die? Was that what was going to happen tonight? And if so, what was the man waiting for?

No. No, she wouldn't even think it. Dying was a beastly thing, and she wouldn't think it.

It was then that Evie noticed what Mr. Anderson's

left hand was doing. It was still holding on to the salt-shaker, and she saw that it was slowly and methodically unscrewing the cap. Maybe . . .

"Sir," she said, looking over at the man, "those are awfully neat glasses. They're like perfect mirrors."

The man stared at her.

"Can I see them?" She opened her eyes wide and gave him a small smile. It was a foolish attempt, or so she thought, but the man, after another pause, removed the glasses and passed them over to her. She looked into his pale blue eyes. They were hard and cold, like a layer of ice on a field of snow. She wondered why he felt he needed to wear the glasses at all. His eyes were just as inscrutable as, and indeed far more intimidating than, the glasses.

Which she glanced down at now. They weren't particularly interesting. She just hoped she had guessed right.

"Excuse me," said Mr. Anderson, and the man turned to look at him. With the same speed with which he had gone to help his wife earlier in the evening, Mr. Anderson's arm shot forward. The contents of the open saltshaker flew into the man's face and he doubled over, holding his eyes and making a strange gurgling grunting sound as he did.

Just as quickly as her husband had done, Mrs.

Anderson grabbed the gun and daggers and was up on her feet. Mr. Anderson barreled into the man, pushing him off his chair and onto the floor.

"Go now!" he shouted, and Mrs. Anderson was quickly at Evie's side, pulling her to her feet.

"Run to the door," she ordered in a fierce whisper.

Evie lurched forward, not entirely aware of her surroundings and stunned by the sudden speed and athleticism of the mild-mannered Andersons. Mrs. Anderson's firm hand was between her shoulder blades, pushing her faster than she could keep pace with. She tripped in the hall and staggered toward the door. Mrs. Anderson yanked it open. Standing in the dark on the threshold was another man. Evie had only a moment to take stock of his terrifying face, which seemed as if it was half melted off—including his ear—before she was yanked back inside by Mrs. Anderson. The melted man lunged and she closed the door just as he did, holding it with her back up against it. She stared wide-eyed at Evie. Then yelled, "Get down!"

Without a thought, Evie flung herself onto the ground as an explosion occurred above her. There was a scuffle behind her, another explosion. Evie wrapped her arms around her head and pressed her face into the cold marble floor. Her whole body was shaking now. She wanted to look, wanted to see what was going on.

"Evie," someone whispered hoarsely.

She couldn't move. She wouldn't move.

"Evie. Get up now."

With all the bravery she could muster she slowly pushed herself to her knees and raised her head. Mrs. Anderson was on the floor, sitting against the door, holding her shoulder. Evie saw red leaking out between her fingers.

"Mrs. Anderson!" she exclaimed, and was up and running over to her.

"No, no, Evie, not now. I'm fine." She winced just as she said it.

"You're not." Evie was full-out panicking now. What could she do? How could she fix this?

"I am. It's only my shoulder. You need to listen to me very carefully." Evie stared at the wound and then looked at Mrs. Anderson's face. The woman's expression was determined. Evie nodded. "Good girl. Now, I need you to reach into my pocket. Do it quickly. There's a letter." Evie slid right up to her and reached into Mrs. Anderson's trouser pocket. Her hand grasped some paper and she withdrew it. She stared at it, an open cream envelope with the Andersons' address handwritten upon it. A couple of drops of ink beside the *A* indicated it had been written in a hurry. Evie flipped it over, and on the back was a broken red wax seal.

"We got this last week. We don't know when it was sent, if it's even real. We didn't want to alarm you. Or give you false hope. But now, with these men here, we know the truth."

"The truth?" Evie was more confused than ever.

Mrs. Anderson held up her hand to silence her and turned her head. "Do you smell that?"

Evie sniffed at the air. A faint bitter smell hit her. It smelled . . . dangerous.

"Fire. Help me up."

Evie jumped to her feet and helped Mrs. Anderson to stand. It was at that point that Evie had a good look around. Mr. Anderson and the man were nowhere to be seen—or heard, for that matter. But the hallway looked like some kind of war zone: a vase smashed on the floor, dirt smeared across the tiles. The sideboard was also overturned.

"Where's Mr. Anderson?" Evie asked.

"I'm sure Ted's fine. Follow me."

Evie followed quickly behind Mrs. Anderson to the rear of the home, through the taupe kitchen toward the small conservatory extension, but from where they stood they could easily see flames on the other side of the glass.

"Then there's only one way about it," said Mrs. Anderson, more to herself than to Evie. "Come with me; we're going to the basement."

Unfinished, dark, dank, an afterthought, the Andersons' basement did not help ease Evie's dread. She followed Mrs. Anderson over to the far end, where flat packs of brown cardboard filled with shelves yet to be assembled leaned against the wall.

"Help me move them," said Mrs. Anderson, and Evie did, more than aware that her hostess was in considerable pain.

Revealed behind the flat packs was a small hole in the wall. It looked like something a person was meant to crawl through, but it was certainly not large enough for that.

"What is this?"

"Once upon a time we were working on a secret passage to outside."

"Why?" Evie asked, when what she really wanted to ask was "Why on earth would people as boring as you need a secret passage?" Although she supposed the Andersons didn't seem quite so boring anymore.

"It was dangerous; then it stopped being dangerous."

Stopped? It had only just begun! "It's dangerous now."

Mrs. Anderson nodded. "It isn't large enough for me, but it is for you."

Evie peered into the hole. "Are you sure about that?"

"Yes. One of the neighbor kids got in last year this way. You need to go now, Evie. Take the letter. Get help."

"Take it where? Where do I get help?" Evie was starting to panic. What was going on, and why was she suddenly the one who had to fix everything?

Mrs. Anderson said the name of a place, and Evie furrowed her brow. She didn't recognize it. Was she supposed to know this place? Did everyone else know about it? Was this yet something else she'd missed out on?

"Go, Evie!" ordered Mrs. Anderson, interrupting her thoughts.

"Okay," Evie said. But no. She couldn't. She couldn't just leave Mrs. Anderson in a house on fire with two dangerous men after her. "You could try to come with me!"

"I won't make it, but I'll be fine. We are always fine. That's what being us means."

"I don't understand. *What* does being you mean?"

"There isn't enough time!"

No, Evie wasn't about to let everything stay all mysterious when so much was being asked of her. "You had enough time to explain about the neighbor kid, you had enough time to move the packs away from the hole, you had enough time—"

"For crying out loud, Evie! I don't want you knowing anything in case you get caught!"

That stunned Evie into silence. Which was convenient, as it meant neither of them could possibly miss the loud crashing noise that followed from somewhere above.

"Go!"

Evie nodded as she turned and faced the hole in the wall. She took a deep breath and then climbed inside. For the first time she could appreciate why there were people in the world who were claustrophobic. The space around her hardly was a space, and she wondered how there could possibly be enough room for both her and air. She had to kind of swim along the tunnel, pulling with her arms, pushing with her legs. She went as fast as she could, but it was difficult. The dirt gave way as she pushed her foot against it, and she would face-plant, getting a mouthful of the stuff.

Evie pushed and pushed and kept going. The crumpled envelope in her hand helped motivate her, and the fear of what she had left behind, of a hand grabbing at her ankle or the tunnel collapsing on her head, helped just a little bit as well.

Then eventually she drew in a breath, and it wasn't just stale dirt she tasted, but a tiny bit of something bright and fresh. Evie pressed forward and the smell got cleaner and crisper, until the tunnel in front of her wasn't quite as dark, and then there was no tunnel at all. She crawled out into the open and took a long, deep inhalation of night air. Then she climbed to her feet. She was dirty, confused, and scared, but she was still alive.

Alive and totally lost.

Evie had no idea where she was other than some-where in the Andersons' neighborhood—the houses looked similar. She looked around and decided that if she tried, she could find her school. Sirens approached,

and instinctively she pressed herself up against a rough brick wall as fire trucks whizzed past. She wanted to follow them, to see the rescue of the Andersons, to see they were okay. But just as the thought entered her mind, a sinister shadow crossed her path. The shadow, a moment later, was revealed to belong to the melted-face man. He walked quickly down the street, and she held her breath as he passed; then she peered around the corner to follow his movements. He stopped a few feet away and twitched his head slightly. Had she made a noise? Was he even looking for her?

She squeezed the letter in her hand, not really thinking why, and held her breath again.

The man picked up his quick stride again and was off down the street and out of sight. Immediately Evie darted across the street in the other direction and began to run. She didn't know where she was going; she only knew she had to get far away from the Andersons' home and the terrifying man. She maneuvered through darkened streets, steering clear of streetlights. She ran down a dark alley that opened onto a narrow road that took her along backyards and driveways. Eventually she came to a garden that backed onto a kitchen, the windows of which were alight. A happy-looking family sat inside playing a board game at the table. She crouched by the back door, and in the porch light looked down at the envelope in her hand.

She opened it and she started to read.

Dear Ted and Trudy,

Despite the rumors, and I daresay many concrete facts, I am not, nor have I ever been, dead. I am, however, in a dire and dangerous situation right now, one from which I fear I cannot extricate myself. I need help. I need someone to come and rescue me. But that is not the worst of it. There are people looking for the key. You must protect it first and foremost. If it is destroyed, my very life could be over, and if it falls into the wrong hands, I cannot even begin to imagine the damage that might occur. Even before you find a way to help me, this must be done. Please.

I know I'm asking a lot of the two of you— you neither desired nor sought an adventurous life. But remember this: the journey is not so treacherous once you understand that the four directions all point home.

Yours in friendship,
Alistair Drake

P.S. If there is any way to send my love to little Evie, please see it done.

Some might find it surprising that of all the information that stood out to Evie in this moment, "send my love to little Evie" hit her in her gut first. But I hope you will agree with me that she could be forgiven in this moment of such distress to thrill to the knowledge that she was loved by someone. And I think we can agree that her indulging the feeling for a moment before considering the real pressing issue of her grandfather's being alive and in grave danger didn't mean she was a selfish creature.

Oh yes. Grandfather. A grandfather Evie had heard mentioned only a handful of times by her father. Her father had always valiantly tried to praise him, but there'd been a tinge of bitterness to his voice, and Evie kind of understood. After all, he had barely been around for his son. For most of her father's life, her grandfather had been out on wild adventures. Adventures Evie had longed to hear tales about. She had wished so much that her grandfather were still alive so he could tell her himself. But he had died years before she was born. Or at least . . . that was what her father had always told her.

When she was younger, Evie had been secretly sad not to have any grandparents, or aunts and uncles, or cousins. She'd never dared say so aloud, though. Her parents had always tried to make their situation seem special. It was just the three of them, a team. And that had been a nice thought. Once. The last couple of years, it had only made her feel completely alone.

But now she wasn't alone. Now she had someone. A grandfather. Her grandfather. The only family she had left. And he was in a dire situation of some kind. And he needed someone to protect a key. And to then rescue him. Probably from the very men she'd just escaped from. She had to help him. There was no question about it.

Yes, she faced a bit of a challenge, considering she didn't know where said key was. Or where her grandfather was. Or why he had asked the Andersons, of all people, for help in the first place. But thanks to Mrs. Anderson, Evie did know now whom to ask for assistance. And that, at least, was an excellent place to start.

She recalled Mrs. Anderson's words and stood, determined.

It was not back to the Wayward School for her. No, not while her only living relative needed her help!

It was, instead, to some place she'd never heard of before, a place that somehow had the answers she was looking for.

Some place called The Explorers Society.

➤ CHAPTER 8 ◄

In which
Sebastian meets Evie.
Or
Evie meets Sebastian.
Or
They meet each other.

The next day after school, Sebastian arrived armed and ready at The Explorers Society. Having stayed up well past his bedtime doing his research, he had determined who each of the five was. And had quickly become profoundly impressed by all of them.

From what Sebastian could tell, Alistair Drake was their leader. He seemed quite sophisticated, based on the formal way he posed in every picture and the fact that he seemed to wear a tweed suit no matter what the weather. He also had a neatly trimmed beard. He was interviewed the most when articles were about the general team. That was what made Sebastian suspect he was the man in charge.

Next was Catherine Lind. She was always photographed with animals and, though she bore a stern expression, seemed very relaxed with them. It was only in photographs with humans that she appeared awkward. She was tall, very tall, which was neither here nor there, but Sebastian couldn't help noting it. She was definitely taller than anyone else in the group. And she wore her hair in a short, sharp bob that ended at her equally sharp cheekbones.

The oldest member of the group was the complete opposite of Catherine, though for some reason she was usually photographed standing next to her in team photos, which only drew attention to how different they were. Her name was Doris Sullivan, and she had long silver hair that she wore in braids usually collected together in a hair tie. She was short and stout and tended to look a little confused as to why she was posing for a picture. It was hard to determine what her role was, but she was often seen underneath various vehicles, so Sebastian thought maybe she was a mechanic.

From the oldest member of the team to the youngest: the Kid didn't seem to have a name, though he must have had one. He was only ever referred to by this nickname. Sebastian thought it was a bit silly, really—he wasn't fond of nicknames as a rule. What

was the point of having another name when one's current name did the job? In any event, the Kid didn't
seem to do much more than rappel down the sides of
mountains and drive fast cars. What his usefulness to
the team could possibly have been eluded Sebastian,
but his fearlessness was nonetheless impressive.

The fifth member was Benedict Barnes—a man
Sebastian almost forgot about, as he was in so few
photographs. This was, of course, because he was the
team's photographer (and cartographer) and thus usually on the other side of the lens. It was also suggested
in one article that the man kept a journal about all
their adventures, but that book was definitely nowhere
to be found in the plain wooden box.

From what Sebastian did find in the box, though,
he was able to learn a lot about the Filipendulous Five.
It seemed that twenty years ago, they had been incredibly famous. Alistair Drake was featured on faded yel-
lowing covers of *Time* magazine not once but twice.
There were pictures of the group with various world
leaders, and there were several of the Kid with different
Hollywood starlets who Sebastian assumed had been
a big deal back in the day. It struck Sebastian as truly
odd that he had never heard of the Filipendulous Five.
Well, he understood why he'd never heard of them out

in the world—after all, two decades had passed since they'd been a big deal, and people move on, find new heroes and celebrities. But explorers from over a century ago were still commemorated at the society headquarters. And there seemed to be no pictures of the Filipendulous Five anywhere, not even in the Hall of Portraits. None of the members ever mentioned them. Why was that? And why had the Filipendulous Five stopped exploring? *Had* they stopped exploring?

What exactly had happened to them, and where were they now?

The closest thing Sebastian got to an answer was a ten-year-old article in the *New Yorker* he'd found online called "The Filipendulous Five: What Exactly Happened to Them, and Where Are They Now?" which, yes, you'd think might have been marginally helpful in answering those questions, but it was merely an article of speculation as to why the team had disbanded, with no concrete evidence to support any of the theories. Pages of different experts sharing their thoughts, each more fantastic than the next. There was talk of Alistair secretly being a pirate and wanting the others to join him and them refusing. Another fellow believed so strongly that the team had had their memories erased and no longer remembered they once

had worked together that he wrote an entire book entitled *Twelve Steps to Not Having Your Brain Wiped*.
Two experts agreed that whatever had happened to
cause the breakup, it must have had something to do
with the Bermuda Triangle, while a third argued that it
had everything to do with the Canadian Quadrangle.

In conclusion, there was simply no single answer to
the question. And most of the time, the experts seemed
more interested in sharing their own personal experience with the Filipendulous Five than anything else.
Only one expert seemed to have any kind of reasonable explanation.

Myrtle Algens.

Sebastian had stopped short when he'd read
that. *Myrtle?* As in, president of The Explorers Society Myrtle? His heart pumped faster as he read on.
Her name wasn't in the article itself, but in a small
sidebar with the heading SOMETIMES THE SIMPLEST
EXPLANATIONS. . . . It read: "But not all believe such
fanciful tales. Myrtle 'The Ice Queen' Algens has a
very straightforward answer to the question. 'They got
tired of each other,' she said. 'After working together
so closely for so many years, they decided enough was
enough. I think the team felt overshadowed by Alistair,
and I think they each wanted to do their own thing.

They changed their names and got on with their lives. It's not a mystery.' "

It was such an unimaginative answer—Sebastian thought it was just beautiful. A perfect moment of logic in an ocean of overly dramatic posturing. It made him like Myrtle even more.

Though . . . it still made him wonder . . . if it wasn't a big deal that they were no longer a team, why was there no evidence they'd ever existed as one in the first place? Why had someone hidden a secret box behind a secret door?

Sebastian had made up his mind that all this speculating was enough. There was only so far you could go with guessing. He decided to go right to the source: Myrtle herself. He would just ask her outright. That was the obvious decision. Plus he did kind of want to show off that he'd done his assignment, that he'd done something inappropriate. He was looking forward to the inevitable praise. Not that Sebastian had followed the rules, or in this case broken them, for the approval. No, he had done it because that was the right thing to do. But approval was a nice by-product. And who didn't like a little "Well done!" every now and then?

And so, at headquarters, after he had completed all his usual chores and his shift was coming to an end, he sought out Myrtle, sticking his head into every room to give it a once-over.[9]

He tried to think of the most logical place to find her as he checked every room. Sebastian snapped his fingers when he finally made the realization. Of course. He changed his direction and made his way up to the roof, and sure enough, he could see Myrtle sitting in the tree in the distance. David Copperfield wandered over to him and Sebastian gave him a quick scratch. Then the cat lay down to sunbathe on the cobblestone path, and Sebastian dashed over to the nearest rope ladder and climbed up to join the society president.

"Hello, Sebastian, and how are you this lovely afternoon?" asked Myrtle with a smile. Even though she looked quite calm, Sebastian noticed that her shirt was rumpled and her hair tousled. She also seemed to be slightly out of breath, and her cheeks flushed. Weird.

"I'm well. In fact, I'm very well."

"Good, good." Myrtle had evidently just finished pouring herself a cup of tea and was sitting back in her seat, holding the teapot on her lap. Sebastian wondered if it was uncomfortable to do so, if it was hot to

---

[9] Except for the once-over room. That was where the oldest members of the society spent their time, and they did not like being disturbed by anyone, especially by Sebastian.

the touch. But Myrtle didn't seem bothered by it. The table was, as always, set for two. But he wasn't sure he should sit and join her.

"I have some news." He couldn't help but smile. He'd been so looking forward to this moment.

"Do you? Please sit," she said, and Sebastian, relieved that the decision was taken away from him, sat.

"I completed my assignment. I did something inappropriate." He smiled brightly and waited for Myrtle to say something lovely about him.

But she didn't. Instead she squinted at him and then, after a moment, shook her head and sighed, focusing on examining a small Fig Newton and peanut butter sandwich.

Well, that hadn't gone as expected. "Uh, so, I wanted to let you know, I guess," said Sebastian awkwardly. "And I also wanted to ask you something."

"Ask away," said Myrtle, taking a bite of the sandwich and then nodding her approval.

"What happened to the Filipendulous Five?"

Myrtle coughed and then spat chewed-up Fig Newton and peanut butter across the table. A little piece landed on Sebastian's nose. "What did you just say?" She stared at him with wide eyes.

"I, uh, I asked what happened to the Filipendulous Five," repeated Sebastian, taken aback. He was so shocked by her reaction that he couldn't move. He just sat there. With chewed-up sandwich on his nose.

"Who told you about the Filipendulous Five? Was it that girl?" Myrtle's voice was severe, threatening. The teapot in her lap shook. Sebastian was sincerely happy that no one had told him about the Filipendulous Five because he was pretty sure they'd be in big trouble. Also, what girl?

"What girl?" he asked.

"Never mind the girl." Myrtle waved the idea of the girl, or any girl, away. "How do you know about them?" she pressed.

For some reason Sebastian suddenly felt really unsure about telling Myrtle the truth. It occurred to him now that maybe the box hadn't just been hidden from the world at large, but from the other explorers in the society too.

"I found an article at the local library about them. I was researching your name. I . . . wanted to learn more about your history of exploration. And this article about what happened to them came up. So I thought I'd ask you myself. In the article you said that they just disbanded, and I was wondering if you really believed that." It was a pretty convincing lie, and quite honestly, Sebastian was uneasy about how effortlessly he'd come up with it.

"Well, I said as much, didn't I?" replied Myrtle, still looking at him in a way that made Sebastian shift uncomfortably in his seat.

"But where are they now? Why are there no pictures of them here? It doesn't make sense. . . ." Sebastian trailed off when he noticed Myrtle's face getting redder and redder. Her whole body—not just the teapot—was shaking now, and he was terrified she was about to go off like a firework, exploding into little sparkly bits of silver and droplets of tea.

"No more of this," she said through clenched teeth. "That chapter is long over. That road has come to an end. The door is locked and the key hidden."

"I . . . don't understand what any of that means . . . ," said Sebastian, feeling distinctly uncomfortable.

"Leave," she said. Sebastian had never quite heard such a tone before. It froze him all the way to his bones. Which made it all the more difficult to do what she was telling him to do. "Leave," she said again, louder this time. David Copperfield meowed in a way that was very "Yeah, you'd better do what she's saying. Like, now."

Sebastian listened to the cat's sage advice and left. Oh boy, did he leave. He sprang down out of the tree, avoiding the ladder altogether, and sprinted along the cobblestone path to the door, and only after he was safely back inside, down the stairs, and with the painting shut behind him did he stop. And wonder: what exactly had just happened?

He continued to wonder as he jumped into the elevator. And then he went from wondering to thinking about it intently as he dodged the pig that Hubert was walking on a leash down the main hall. And finally he changed to pondering as he stepped outside. His pondering was so all-consuming that he didn't even notice the girl until he heard a loud sniff just as he was closing the front door behind him.

Sebastian turned in surprise.

The girl sat in the shadows, her knees propping up her chin, staring out before her into the not-so-vast distance. Into what was, Sebastian estimated, a stretch of empty space about fifteen feet wide with a view of a brick wall.

"Uh, are you okay?" It felt like a dumb question. She was distinctly not okay. No one just sat in the shadows of a dark alley with a sad expression if they were okay.

The girl turned her head slightly and looked at him. Then she turned back. "No."

Sebastian had hoped she'd say what was wrong at that point. But she didn't. Did he really need to ask?

Did he really *want* to ask? Not that he wasn't worried about her, but he'd already had a pretty confusing day and now he was late getting home, and being late just added to his stress. He didn't have time to ask questions of forlorn-looking girls. Then again, he couldn't just walk away after her "No" either.

"What's wrong?" he asked, feeling antsy and hoping the question was easily answered.

"They kicked me out."

I guess not. "Who did?"

She raised her arm and, without looking, pointed at the door.

"They let you in?" he asked in surprise.

"Yeah."

"Then they kicked you out?"

"Yeah."

Sebastian paused for a moment and thought. "Well, that's interesting."

The girl looked at him again, this time maintaining her gaze. For all her sadness, there was a determined spark in her eyes that Sebastian respected. Though it also made him slightly uncomfortable in its intensity.

"Why is that interesting?" she asked.

"Uh, well . . ." Sebastian glanced around, and then, resigned to his current situation, took a seat next to her. "It's just that they don't usually let people in in the first place."

"Oh." The girl sighed. "That's not that interesting, actually."

Sebastian felt marginally insulted. He was pretty confident that he had quite the knack for rating what was and wasn't interesting. "They only let people in if they're special in some way."

The girl looked at Sebastian for a moment, then asked, "Are you special?"

Sebastian thought about it, about the members of the society and all their adventures and unique stories and how he didn't remotely fit in with them. "No," he admitted. "I'm an exception."

"How so?"

"It's a long story. There was a pig. Anyway, the thing is, they let you in. That's interesting. And it's also interesting that after deciding to let you in, they then decided to kick you out. What happened?"

The girl turned her body, leaning her shoulder against the wall, and gave him that intense look again. "I rang the bell. Some old man with white tufts of hair sticking out of his head asked who it was. I told him my name. He let me in. I was taken into this room with a bunch of leather chairs, and somebody gave me some tea, and I was left alone for a bit. And then this woman came along, and she was carrying a teapot, so I thought she was maybe going to pour me more tea, but you could tell she was really mad. She was yelling at the man who let me in; she said that strangers weren't allowed in the society and especially not someone with my name, and he was going on about how he can't be expected to remember everything, and then she actually grabbed me. Here." She touched her upper arm. "She dragged me out of the room and literally threw me out of the building. And she didn't have to do any of that. If she had just asked me to leave . . ." Tears welled in her eyes.

Oh no, no, don't cry, sad girl, don't cry.

"Don't cry."

"Why not?"

"I . . ." Wasn't the answer obvious? "It's not so bad being kicked out of places you don't belong."

The girl rose in a rush of fury and stared down at him, hands on hips. "Don't belong? I was *sent* here! I was *supposed* to come here! You have no idea, no idea at all!"

Sebastian stood up too, standing eye to watering eye with the girl. "You know, I'm just trying to be nice. I'm late. I have to get home. My parents are waiting for me."

The girl stared him down and he didn't flinch. He didn't need to deal with any of this. It wasn't his business, and he didn't like being yelled at. Then suddenly the girl seemed to physically deflate. Her shoulders sank, her face softened, her eyes closed, and she stepped to the side to let him pass. Sebastian felt a little bad walking by her.

As he did he heard her say something.

He knew it was just a ploy to make him stop walking, to manipulate him into asking her what she was saying. And he totally fell for it.

"Sorry, what did you say?" he asked, turning around.

"I said it must be nice," replied the girl.

"Oh, okay." He turned to leave again. Oh, for crying out loud . . . "What must be nice?"

The girl shook her head. "I shouldn't have said that. I'm feeling sorry for myself. Thank you for talking with me." She turned and faced the door to The Explorers Society, staring at it intently, as if with the power of her mind she could will herself inside again.

"What's your name?"

The girl leaned against the door, placing her ear to it. "Evie," she said, squinting in concentration.

"What's so special about 'Evie'?" asked Sebastian, walking back toward her.

She pushed herself off the door and stared at it again. "Nothing." She sighed then. "I've never been any kind of standout. I was once locked inside a classroom for a whole lunch hour because my teacher didn't notice I was still there packing up."

"No, I meant about the name Evie. What's so special about your name that they'd open the door for you? And more importantly, get really angry and kick you out?"

"Oh. Well, I think it's my last name."

"What's your last name?"

Evie took a deep breath, and Sebastian watched her draw the courage to lift her fist. She was going to knock, to try again. She paused, holding her hand aloft, floating in the air.

"Evie?"

"Yes?" she asked softly.

"Your last name, what is it?" Sebastian didn't know why, but his pulse had quickened and he was oddly short of breath.

"Drake." She pulled her fist back and sent it toward the door.

Sebastian caught it midflight.

Evie stared at him wide-eyed.

"We need to talk."

➤ CHAPTER 9 ◄

In which Evie feels hopeless.

He was a twitchy boy, so when he had grabbed her wrist so forcefully, his sudden change in demeanor had caught her off guard. She couldn't even say a quiet "Okay." Evie was so surprised, all she could do was nod, and she found she was walking down one of the leafy streets that surrounded the dark alley. Then she was standing before an attractive semidetached home with a well-tended flower garden in the front.

"My mom finds flowers whimsical," the boy said.

"Whimsical?"

"She says they follow the laws of physics to a point but seem to have rebellious streaks. She likes to pretend flowers have the ability to think. She finds it funny."

"Okay . . ."

Then Evie was in a cozy foyer, standing in awkward silence as the boy called out, "I'm home! I brought a friend."

"Are they staying for dinner?" called out someone she assumed was his father.

The boy looked at Evie and she nodded quickly. Of course she was staying for dinner; she had nowhere else to go.

"Yes!"

Then she was following him up his stairs and was in his room, and it was at that point that her disorientation subsided and the world resumed at a more normal pace. Evie admired the boy's walls, covered in maps from around the world. She reached out and touched an edge that curled up, revealing another map beneath. How many layers were there? How long had he been putting up maps? How nice to be able to have the time to create this kind of a collection, to have layers of something at all. A home to rely on, to invest time in.

Don't feel self-pity, she reprimanded herself. *Don't.*

She watched as the boy sat on the floor and held a box in his lap. He indicated she should join him, so she did.

"What's your name?" she asked—because she still didn't know.

"Sebastian."

"Okay."

He placed the box between them. "Have you seen this before?"

Taking the question with all due seriousness, Evie picked up the box and examined it closely. She didn't really have to, though. She didn't remember any time in her life when a box had been a part of it. Even when she'd moved into the school, she'd packed her one bag and that was all. Boxes were not something she'd had relationships with.

"No." She put it down.

Sebastian performed a series of movements with the box. He did it so quickly, she couldn't really follow. Somehow he opened it with so much enthusiasm that the contents went spilling out between them. Papers and photographs, all weathered with age. Evie picked up a newspaper article with a picture of a handsome young man dangling off the edge of a cliff.

It was snatched from her hand and replaced with a photograph of a group of five people.

"Do you recognize anyone?" asked Sebastian.

Evie held the photograph close and examined each person in the picture.

"No."

"No? Are you sure?"

"Pretty sure." She tried to hand the photograph back to Sebastian, but he pushed it back in her direction.

"Not even him?" he pointed at an older gentleman with a neatly trimmed beard. He was dressed in a tweed suit and had his hand on the shoulder of the young man she'd seen in the article just before.

"No. Who is he?"

Sebastian sighed in disappointment. "His name is Alistair Drake. I thought maybe . . . But of course that was stupid of me. Not everyone who has the same last name is related."

Evie felt a flutter of excitement in her chest. "But I *am*! I *am* related to Alistair Drake. He's my grandfather! I've just never met him is all. Wait, this is him?" She looked closer at the picture. Now she could see beyond the lined face and the beard to the friendly twinkle in the eye, that mischievous spark that had always been the prelude to adventuring. Not his twinkle, though. Her father's. Being woken up at three in the morning: "Do you want to see something amazing?" And standing outside on their lawn watching the northern lights dance across the sky.

He had her father's eyes. Or, she supposed, her father had Alistair Drake's eyes. And there were other things too. The long fingers, the straight back, the high forehead.

"Where did you find this?" she asked, not realizing she was whispering.

"At the society headquarters. It was hidden in the back of a filing cabinet, inside a secret door."

"Really?" She touched her grandfather's face. This kind face. It was in trouble now. Not smiling now. And he needed her help. Evie looked up at Sebastian with concern. "He's in danger."

"Who, your grandfather?"

"Yes." She pulled out the letter and handed it to Sebastian. For a brief moment she wondered if she should trust him so easily, but it was too late anyway. She hoped her instincts were right.

Sebastian read over the letter. "When did you get this?"

"Last night. Mrs. Anderson gave it to me. In the tunnel. She . . . might be dead now." Evie stared down at her hands folded in her lap. She closed her eyes. It wasn't grief she was feeling, but a huge overwhelming guilt.

"Dead? Tunnel? Evie, what's going on?"

She kept her eyes closed, squeezing them as tightly as she could. "There were these two men, and then a fire, and then I escaped in a tunnel. And I know they were looking for something, and I think I know what it is."

"The key mentioned in the letter?" asked Sebastian.

Evie nodded. He was a smart one, that was for sure. "And I was told to go to The Explorers Society for help, only they didn't."

"I'm . . . sorry." Sebastian sounded far off, as if he were fading away. Evie opened her eyes. No, he was still sitting just there. He looked concerned and also frightened. She instantly felt even more terrible for distressing him like that.

"No, *I'm* sorry. It's none of your concern. I shouldn't have said anything."

"But you should go to the police or something, shouldn't you?"

"I guess."

"You guess?"

"I think there's something really big going on," said Evie, "bigger than the police. If my grandfather is in some kind of dire situation with these men but he's more worried about this key than his own safety, then I think there's a reason not to get the police involved."

Sebastian furrowed his brow and nodded. "Yeah.

Though I really hope that reason isn't that he's doing something illegal," he said.

"Me too. But even if it was, do I want my grandfather found and then arrested?"

"Well, if he's doing something bad . . ."

"He's the one who's in trouble! These men have him prisoner or something and his life is on the line!"

"I'm just trying to help."

"Are you?" Evie realized only then that she was up on her feet. How had that happened? She noticed too that the picture in her hand was shaking. No. Not the picture. It was her hand. No. Not her hand. It was her whole body.

Sebastian was staring up at her, and once again she felt bad for getting upset with him. It wasn't his fault. He was making good, appropriate suggestions. It just felt like . . . well, sometimes, in some moments, at some times, good, appropriate suggestions could be the most inappropriate suggestions to suggest.

"Why does everyone think I'm not trying to help when I am so clearly attempting to do just that?" Sebastian didn't say it in a defensive tone. It almost sounded a little sad.

"I'm sorry for getting upset with you," she replied, sitting down again. "But I just don't think we should call the police, and since he's my grandfather and not yours, I hope you respect my wishes."

Sebastian didn't say anything for a moment, and then nodded. "Okay."

Evie took in a deep breath and calmed herself down. She looked at the picture again and felt even more certain that she needed to rescue her grandfather. She'd never felt more right about anything in her life, even though she hadn't the first idea how one orchestrated a rescue mission. But before all that, she did need to protect this key. It was what he had requested, and she was going to show him she could be counted on.

"What now?" asked Sebastian.

"I have to find the key and protect it. I have to do it for him. The good news is I'm pretty sure the men last night were looking for the key, and that means they don't know where it's hidden yet either."

"How can you be so sure?" asked Sebastian.

"When the first man arrived, Mr. Anderson said something like 'It's not here,' so the men must have been making a guess. And guessed wrong. Though why they guessed it was at the Andersons' I have no idea. Why else would they go somewhere where a thing was not?"

She watched Sebastian think about that and then nod. "Makes sense."

"So I think that gives us some time to find it, hopefully before those men do. But how?" Evie inched herself closer to the rest of the papers, putting down the picture and starting to riffle through the rest. She could sense Sebastian still watching her, but finally he shifted and started pushing through some of the papers himself. "I don't suppose it's here," she said, picking up a different photograph of her grandfather, this time of him playing a game of chess opposite a monkey.

Sebastian shook his head. "I've been through everything thoroughly. No key. Just papers."

Evie sighed. "Well, maybe there's a clue. . . ."

"You really think so?" said Sebastian.

"You said the box was hidden. And so is this key. There has got to be a connection there." Evie reached over and picked up another piece of paper. It was an article about Catherine Lind's Great African Parrot Rescue.

"What happens when we find it?"

"I don't know. Maybe there'll be a clue with it about what it opens. Maybe some kind of information telling us where these men are keeping my grandfather, or at least why he's in trouble. Maybe when we find it we'll figure out how to rescue him!"

She started to go through the papers more quickly, picking one up and looking it over, putting it down, picking up another. It was difficult to tell what was important and what wasn't. So many stories, so many adventures. Each one unique, each one involving derring-dos and doing dares. There was a villain for every story: poachers in Belize, CEOs of large oil companies trying to shut down small villages, thieves and tricksters. Blackmailers. But all had been overcome. All had gotten their just deserts. As had the Filipendulous Five, celebrating victories with their own after-dinner treats—usually, it seemed, ice-cream sundaes.

"If only we could just ask someone at The Explorers Society," said Evie, feeling quite frustrated by now.

"Yeah, why do they have to be so weird about it?" replied Sebastian, reading over an article.

"They are the only ones who might know where he is. The only ones who could possibly help us find this key. And they completely refuse. They wouldn't even let me tell them why I was there, or show them the letter!" Evie threw down a paper and folded her arms across her chest. She had made herself all angry again.

"Something pretty big must have happened once upon a time," said Sebastian. "I tried asking Myrtle about it and she told me to leave!"

"They're all scared. Too scared to help. When they are the only ones with the answer!" It was so unfair.

Why was she, a girl of eleven, braver than a bunch of risk-taking explorers?

"No," said Sebastian suddenly, and Evie looked at him. His eyes were shining bright, and he looked excited.

"No?" she said, not exactly sure what he was saying no to.

"They aren't the only ones who might know something."

"But who else would?" asked Evie. "Who is this one special person who isn't a member of The Explorers Society and yet somehow happens to know where my grandfather might be and why?"

"Not one person," said Sebastian, holding up the group photograph. "Four."

➤ CHAPTER 10 ◄

In which a plan is made.

It was possibly the most dramatic thing Sebastian had ever said, and he wasn't entirely sure he felt comfortable with himself for saying it that way. He also now felt a little guilty that he hadn't just simply said "I think the most logical thing to do would be to see if we can find one of the other four of the Filipendulous Five and ask them if they know anything about the key and your grandfather" instead of his mysterious "No." It seemed pretty mean, now that he thought about it, prolonging Evie's pain and frustration just for the satisfaction of presenting his idea in as theatrical a way as possible.

It also kind of freaked him out because being theatrical went against Sebastian's nature, but it felt good to see Evie's sad eyes widen and a smile stretch across her face. She bounced up and gave him a big hug of gratitude, and he couldn't help but smile a little also.

"Yes! Of course, yes! Sebastian, that's a brilliant idea! And so obvious. Why didn't I think of it?" said Evie. "We have to find one of the others—they'll know! And then we'll find the key, and then I'll go find my grandfather, and then, finally, I'll be . . ." She stopped short.

"You'll be what?"

"Oh. Never mind. It's okay." Evie looked down and scrunched up her face in a weird way he didn't understand, and then looked at him once again. "So how do we find any of them?"

"Kids, dinnertime!" called Sebastian's father.

The two of them looked at each other, and Sebastian for the first time in his life felt annoyed with his parents for interrupting such an important moment. "I guess we'll have to figure that out after we eat," he replied, reluctantly standing up.

It was then that he finally realized it wasn't like they had a lot of time in the first place. Evie surely had to go home at some point. Now that he thought about it, why weren't her parents helping her find her grandfather? Surely he mattered as much to them as he did to Evie. Sebastian was struck that his own personal excitement about the situation could have caused him to not question something that was so obvious.

He turned to Evie, but she had already left the room, and he followed her quickly downstairs to join his mother and father in the dining room.

"Well, Evie," said Sebastian's father as he began methodically cutting all his peas in half after introductions had been made, "and do you go to school with Sebastian?"

Evie nodded easily. "Yes, I do."

This surprised Sebastian, as that was not the case at all, and he looked at Evie, who refused to make eye contact.

"And what's your interest?" asked his mother, passing Sebastian the pepper before he could ask for it.

"My interest?" asked Evie.

"Yes—math, chemistry, physics . . ."

"Oh," said Evie. "I suppose history."

Sebastian stopped peppering and stared at her and then at his mother, who looked terribly confused.

"Yes, Evie likes history a lot, which is why I wanted to show her my maps. But her *interest* is in biology," said Sebastian quickly and a little too loudly.

Evie looked at him then and seemed to understand that she should play along. "Oh, I see," she said with a laugh, "you meant my *interest*! I thought you meant what I was interested in. Oh yes, biology. I do love biology."

"Ah! That makes sense." Sebastian's father's expression brightened. "Are you also interested in being a doctor, like our Sebastian here?" he asked.

"I'm more interested in the biology of animals," said Evie, not missing a beat. "We're studying the life cycle of the fruit fly right now. Fascinating stuff."

"It is, it is," replied his mother, and Sebastian realized only then how upright and stiff he'd been holding himself. He breathed out and allowed himself to relax a little.

"I also wanted to thank you all for letting me stay here while my parents are out of town," said Evie, and Sebastian felt his whole body instantly tense again. What? Since when? They were?

Sebastian's parents both froze and turned their gaze to their son. He gave them a little smile, hoping it looked like an apology for not asking when really it was the only thing he would ever think of doing in the situation.

"Of course," said his father slowly, turning back to Evie. "It's our pleasure."

"It's so nice of you! Could you pass the potatoes, please?"

The potatoes were passed.

The remainder of the meal was decidedly uneventful. Though with all the questions churning about in Sebastian's brain, not to mention the challenge of finding one of the Filipendulous Five to help them, it also felt interminable. More small talk was made about fruit flies, there was a discussion about the metric system, and his mother told the joke about the two salamanders, which Sebastian had never found particularly funny. Finally the main course was done, and as quickly as he could, Sebastian excused himself and Evie, skipping dessert, and they hurried back to his room.

"What are you doing?" he asked, closing the door behind them.

"What? What do you mean?" She looked completely confused by the question.

"Why did you say that about staying over?" Sebastian pressed. "Why did you say that about your parents?"

"Oh," said Evie, sitting on the floor once more. "I needed a place to stay. I didn't mean to lie."

"I think you did, though," replied Sebastian. He watched as she began going through the papers again.

"Well, of course I meant to, but I didn't mean anything bad by it. This is hopeless!" She sat upright and leaned against the foot of his bed. "There's nothing new here. We've been through it all. Let's go on the computer!" She stood up and made for his desk, but Sebastian stepped in front of her.

"Stop," he said. Evie stopped and looked at him with a puzzled expression. "Evie, what's going on? What happened? Why do you need a place to stay? And what was all that about an attack earlier?" He was getting mad at himself for having been so distracted by the excitement of the mystery earlier that he hadn't asked the most straightforward of questions.

Evie sighed hard. "Can we not? Let's just see if we can find where the rest of the Filipendulous Five are instead." She tried to sidestep him, but he moved with her. She sighed again. "I don't want to talk about it."

"Well, you have to. I don't really know you, and I might have been drawn in by everything earlier, but now I'm aware of how strange it all is. You've done a good job telling me just enough so I think you've told me something, but it's not true. You've told me nothing. And I need to know what's going on. Tell me." He put his hands on his hips. Yes, maybe he had enjoyed indulging his moment of theatrics earlier, but this was too much now. It was time for some plain talking.

For the third time Evie sighed. She walked over to the window, then turned, leaning her back against the radiator beneath it. She stared at him for a moment longer. "Last night," she said, "I was at my weekly dinner with the Andersons when a man came to the door and held us hostage. We attempted to escape, but there was another man. And then I don't know what happened, but a gun was fired and Mrs. Anderson was hurt, and the house was set on fire, and then I was sent through a secret tunnel. But before I left, Mrs. Anderson gave me the letter from my grandfather and told me to go to The Explorers Society and ask for help." She looked down at her hands for a moment, took a deep breath, and then looked up at him again. Her eyes were shining.

"My parents died two years ago in a car accident," she continued. "My grandfather's the only family I have left. I didn't even know he was still alive until Mrs. Anderson gave me the letter. I have nowhere to go except back to the school where I was sent by the state. And if I go back there, then I know I can't go save my grandfather. And then I'll really be alone and then there will be no one in the whole world who . . . who . . ."

Sebastian watched her struggle to hold herself together and felt really bad for her. He also felt really uncomfortable. He had asked her to tell him all this, yes, but he hadn't quite expected a story so harrowing.

"Yes?" he urged softly.

She looked down again, and soft waves of hair fell

in front of her face, obscuring it. "Who loves me," she finished.

Well, Sebastian certainly did not know what to say to that.

Evie sniffed and then raised her head in a defiant kind of way. She quickly wiped her face with her hands and said simply, "And that's why I have to stay here until I know how to find the key in the letter, and how to find a way to help my grandfather. And that's why I lied to your parents. I'm sorry."

Sebastian nodded solemnly. "Well," he said slowly, still trying to wrap his head around everything he'd just heard, "I'm sorry you had to deal with that." He approached her carefully and placed a hand on her shoulder. "Of course you can stay here until we find out where the key is."

"And my grandfather."

Sebastian wasn't sure about that. Finding a key was one thing; finding someone in a dangerous situation was quite another. He didn't know if they could actually do that.

"Yes," said Sebastian, astonished that he would say something so certain when he felt anything but. "Step one, find the key. Step two, find a way to help your grandfather."

Evie looked at him with one of her totally unreadable

expressions. And then suddenly she smiled, and it felt like the sun breaking through dark storm clouds, and Sebastian felt a wave of relief wash over him.

"Just, I mean, let me in on the lie next time, okay?" he asked, flashing her his own smile.

Evie laughed. "Deal." She stuck out her hand and Sebastian took it. They shook. "Okay, so where do we start, do you think?"

"Well, the only one whose possible whereabouts I know of is the Kid. There was an article about how he wanted to work in Hollywood when he was done with all the exploring. I mean, whether or not he followed through . . ." He sank back down and dug through the papers.

"Hollywood is pretty far away," said Evie, sounding a little disappointed.

"Yeah, maybe as a last resort . . ." Sebastian didn't really want to think about how they would handle traveling that far. "I think . . ." He sat up and stared at the papers in front of him. "Can you pass me your grandfather's letter?" Evie nodded and did so.

Sebastian stared at it hard. It felt wrong that the letter would have so little information in it when it was asking so much of them. He read it over again. And another time. And a third time.

"What's this business about the different directions

pointing to home? How can different directions do that? They each lead somewhere else," he said.

Evie furrowed her brow at him, so Sebastian leaned forward, showing her the spot, and she read the line. "Oh yeah. I forgot about that bit." She took the letter from his hand, rereading that line. She looked up and seemed to be thinking hard, gazing off somewhere beyond his right shoulder. Sebastian watched her, fascinated by her intensity yet again. And then her eyes seemed to focus. She was no longer gazing off; she was staring at something. Sebastian turned and looked. All he could see was his wall.

Evie stood up and crossed the room. She placed her finger on the wall, and under her finger there happened to be a map.

"New Zealand?"

"Sebastian!" Evie said in frustration.

"What? That's a map of New . . ." He stopped and looked closer. Her finger was on a small *N* in the bottom corner. Suddenly he understood. " 'Four directions all point home.' North, south, east, west. Of course! Like directions on a map! What do you think it means? Do we have to find a map as well now?"

Evie darted back across the room and sat on the floor. Sebastian joined her and they went back through the papers. He wasn't sure how the idea of a map would make finding a key any easier, but it was something more than they'd had a minute ago. After a few more minutes of riffling through the papers, however, their enthusiasm for maps had waned. The new piece of information didn't seem to make their task any easier. So many photographs of so many interesting people and places and yet not one clue ... "So many photographs," Sebastian said slowly.

"Yes?" asked Evie, looking up.

"Benedict Barnes."

"What about him?"

"He was their photographer and kept a journal."

"Okay ..."

"But he was also the cartographer." He looked up at Evie, who was staring back at him wide-eyed.

"Maybe ... maybe he's the one who has the key ...," said Evie, slowly smiling.

"Exactly. Maybe that part of the letter is a clue directing us to find him!" said Sebastian, smiling too. Her enthusiasm was infectious.

"But how do we do that?"

"Well, let's start by sorting out everything in this pile that's about him."

Evie nodded and the two of them got to work.

It didn't take them very long, as there were so few pictures of him and most articles generally talked about Alistair, Catherine, or the Kid. Once they'd collected their small pile, they split it in two and looked at each item carefully.

Sebastian couldn't find anything. Not one clue to where Benedict might be now. "Well?" he asked when Evie put down her pile.

She sighed. "Nothing."

"Okay, let's use the computer." Sebastian had been avoiding this option because it seemed so obvious and he couldn't believe it would be that easy. But maybe the answer was really that simple.

They both got up and crossed to his desk. Sebastian sat down and Evie stood behind him, holding on to the back of his swivel chair. They searched for Benedict's name. Information popped up. Several articles, in fact. But all were about the past, and most they'd already read.

"Nothing," said Evie again. Sebastian stared at the computer and tried typing in the last name first. Still nothing.

"I wonder if he changed his name," said Evie.

Of course! He thought back to the article and what Myrtle had said in it. "That's probably it." Of course, that would only make things even more difficult.

"Okay, try typing in just his first name but also things like 'photography' and 'geography' and 'cartography' and stuff," said Evie, leaning forward.

Sebastian nodded and typed. What appeared was a list of many different Benedicts who were CEOs of various corporations, a few misspelled reviews of *Much Ado About Nothing,* various maps of towns called Benedict . . .

"Wait, what's that!" Evie pointed. Sebastian didn't have time to see at what, as she let go of his chair and dashed to the floor, grabbing a photograph and coming back. "College University," she said with a grin, and Sebastian looked at the photograph. It was one of the rare ones of Benedict. He was sitting at a desk, working. Next to him was a mug with "College University" written on it.

Sebastian looked at the screen. There was a listing that mentioned a Benedict and College University together. "But I bet a lot of Benedicts have gone to that school."

"Maybe. Check it out," she said. He could feel Evie vibrating with excitement through his chair.

He checked it out.

"It's him!" Evie released the chair so fast that it spun around in a full circle and Sebastian had to grab hold of the desk to stop it.

"It really is," he said, when he had reoriented himself.

Sure enough, staring at them was Benedict's familiar unsmiling face. He was pictured on a page featuring other faculty members of College University. Sebastian read aloud: " 'Benedict Silo has been professor of cartography and geography here at the university for almost twenty years. Before that he was an adjunct and guest lecturer and did both his undergraduate and postdoctorate work here as well.' "

"He's pretty loyal, I guess," said Evie, and Sebastian nodded. "But *Silo*?"

"I can't believe we found him," said Sebastian, still in awe. "Even with a different last name."

"Me neither!" said Evie breathlessly. "Okay, so what's his schedule like?"

A bit more research and they had that information, along with a map of the university, which they printed off. They sat back on the floor, examining it and his schedule.

"He has a class tomorrow at one p.m.! Perfect!" said Evie.

"It is?" Sebastian couldn't figure out what was particularly perfect about a one p.m. class time.

"Yes, we can go find him and talk to him. Maybe even check out his office, too!"

Sebastian was starting to feel distinctly uncomfortable. He shifted his position and bit the insides of his cheeks.

"Hey, what's wrong?" Evie was looking at him carefully.

"Oh, nothing. It's just, I can't go tomorrow. So I guess . . . I guess you have to go on your own." Why did that make him feel weird? No, not weird . . . disappointed.

"You have to come with me. I can't do this by myself!" Evie looked aghast at the very suggestion.

Sebastian stared at her. "I have school tomorrow."

"Exactly! It's the perfect cover."

It was suddenly dawning on him. "Wait. You want me to skip school?"

"Yes, of course."

His breath was getting shallow. "I can't skip school."

"Why not?"

"It's not a thing you can do," he said, feeling his heart racing. "You don't just not go to school. It's wrong. And besides, I could miss something important."

"What, like the meaning of life or something?" laughed Evie. "I think that would take more than one afternoon to teach. Besides, tomorrow is Friday. No one ever teaches anything interesting on a Friday."

So now it appeared he was hyperventilating.

"Sebastian, are you okay?"

"I think so. I might be having a panic attack, but other than that I'm okay." He concentrated hard on slowing down his breathing.

"Oh, Sebastian, I'm sorry. I didn't realize this was such a big deal for you. No, of course you don't have to come. I can do it. This is my personal quest anyway. You shouldn't have to be involved." She sounded sincere, if a little sad.

Sebastian shook his head. "No, I promised I'd help you find the key. I'll come tomorrow. It'll be fine. And then we'll find Benedict and you'll have the answer and then I'll go back to school on Monday and catch up." He took in another slow breath. "I've done it before. Those times I've been sick and had to stay home.

I always catch up. Though sometimes I wonder if I'd have been a better artist if I hadn't missed coloring in unicorns that day in kindergarten."

Suddenly he felt arms wrapped around him, squeezing whatever breath remained in him out in one tight hug. "Oh, thank you, thank you! You won't regret this, I promise!" said Evie.

"You're welcome," wheezed Sebastian. "Could you . . . release me now, please?"

"Of course!" Evie let him go and just stared at him, smiling wide.

"It's uh . . . probably time for us to turn in," said Sebastian, feeling a little uncomfortable with how grateful she looked.

"Okay! So the plan for tomorrow will be we say we're going to school, but really we'll get on the bus and head to the university. I think we'll have plenty of time to get there by one." Evie stood up and so did Sebastian.

"Good plan," said Sebastian, realizing just then that not only would he be skipping school, but he'd have to lie to his parents about it. He really couldn't talk about this anymore; he might black out from the stress. "Here, let me show you to your room."

➤CHAPTER 11◄

In which no dead bodies
are found.

The fact that Sebastian was ready to skip school for her gave Evie a great sense of confidence. She hadn't known him long, but she could definitely see what a sacrifice that was for him, and since he seemed so logical, surely the only reason he'd make one like that was because he thought she was on to something. Because he thought seeking out Benedict Barnes was the right tactic to take. It all seemed to Evie to be a kind of sign. An indication. A gentle, polite nod that she was heading in the proper direction. As she sat on the bed in the guest room of Sebastian's house, buttoning up the top to the pajamas his mother had kindly provided for her (Evie wasn't a fool; she knew how suspicious her lack of luggage looked to them and was grateful for their lack of questions), she thought that maybe, just maybe, for the first time in years, things were looking up.

It was true they didn't know if Benedict would have the key. But it was a start, and even if they were wrong about the key, it was very likely Benedict would have some information, something that could help them. He might even know where her grandfather was! And then she could find him, and rescue him, and then they'd have a firm embrace and he'd say, "You look so much like your father!" Or tell her how brave she was for putting herself in so much danger to save him, something like that. He'd take her home with him, and she'd have a real family again. Just like she'd had once. Like everyone else continued to have. Like Sebastian had.

There was a knock on the guest room door and she popped out of bed to answer it. It was Sebastian, dressed in a pair of rocket ship flannel pajamas. Hers had mathematical equations on them; she imagined they looked quite the team. My goodness, she thought, staring at his freckled face, what would she have done without him? What a nice person this Sebastian was. Really. When you thought about it.

"Hey, I thought you might want to see this," he

said. He seemed a lot calmer than before, which made Evie feel better. "Can I come in?"

"Yeah, of course," she answered, and stepped aside. She closed the door behind him and saw that he had a newspaper in his hand.

Sebastian sat on the bed and opened the newspaper to the second page. "Look," he said, and Evie did. It was today's paper, shortly to be yesterday's paper. Sebastian was pointing at a picture of fire trucks in front of a house, and the headline: ARSON?

Evie pulled the paper toward herself, her heart picking up speed. "That's the Andersons' place," she said. She edged in closer to Sebastian to get a better look at the article.

"Yeah," Sebastian said. "I thought there had to have been something about it written down. Fires are usually pretty newsworthy."

"Usually." She read carefully, her mind racing and fear filling her up.

"Here," he said, and he pointed at a paragraph farther down.

Evie read aloud, " 'No bodies were found in the aftermath, and the fire investigator is saying that it appears the family was away from home.' " When she looked up at Sebastian, he smiled at her.

"See? They aren't dead."

Evie nodded. No bodies were found. That was a good thing. But why did that seem almost scarier?

"Are you okay? I thought that would make you feel better," said Sebastian.

"It does," she said. "I just . . . I wonder what their relationship was with my grandfather, why he'd write to them, of all people."

"Oh, well, I don't know," replied Sebastian, seeming sincerely disappointed he didn't have the answer for her. But she hadn't expected him to.

Evie shook her head and then smiled at Sebastian. "It's okay, never mind that now." She stifled a yawn. "I'm very tired; it's been a very long day. I haven't slept since it all happened."

"Oh wow!" Sebastian looked sincerely astonished. "You stayed up all night?"

"Yeah," she replied, just in that moment realizing how sleepy she was.

"But you need to sleep eight hours every night. Our bodies function best that way," said Sebastian.

Evie nodded. "They also function best when alive. And I was running for my life."

"Oh. Well, yeah. That's important too."

Evie nodded again.

"But you should go to sleep now. I'll leave."

Sebastian stood and crossed back to the door. "Good night!" He gave her a smile.

"Good night," she replied, and lay back on the bed as he closed the door.

No bodies were found.

That was good. It was *really* good. She had to hope that the Andersons were somewhere safe, that they had escaped and maybe were coming up with a plan to find the key and maybe even rescue her grandfather too. Maybe somehow they'd find out where she was and show up first thing tomorrow at Sebastian's front door . . . and . . . It didn't really make sense, but it was nice to hope. Maybe then the Andersons would go to The Explorers Society themselves. Surely they would let them in, since they were the ones who had told her to go there in the first place. Yes! That was a possibility. Maybe it would be all over by tomorrow and she wouldn't have to worry about keys and rescuing her grandfather from some very scary and definitely evil men on her own, or . . .

Evie's eyes widened suddenly and she rolled over onto her side. She squeezed the pillow underneath her tightly. So tightly she thought it might pop in an explosion of feathers. But she didn't care; she needed to hug something right now, hug and hug and hug.

Because it had just occurred to her that if no bodies

were found, then that meant that not only were the Andersons still out there somewhere—so were those two evil men.

And she knew they knew she existed.

And if they had read the papers also . . .

Then they'd know . . . she was still out there somewhere too.

≻ CHAPTER 12 ≺

In which the search begins.

Collage University was located on the east side and existed in a perpetual autumn. Tall Gothic buildings masked by red-, orange-, and yellow-leafed trees were connected by brick paths through green grass. And students with backpacks slung over a shoulder, scarves around their necks, and books in the crooks of their arms walked with some speed from building to building, acknowledging the need to get to class on time but not wanting to look too eager.

Sebastian felt immediately out of place, much in the same way he did at The Explorers Society. Except it was completely different. At The Explorers Society, Sebastian always felt not quite adventurous enough; at the university, Sebastian felt anxious, desperate to be one of the students. Wishing time would speed up so he could finally belong with them, lounging under trees reading books, or rushing this way and that drinking from disposable coffee cups.

Of course, watching everyone going to school did not help settle Sebastian's nerves about skipping going to his own right now. He could feel his chest constricting in panic and his breathing getting shallower. He stopped walking for a second and took in two slow breaths.

"Are you okay?" asked Evie, coming over to him.

"Yes," he replied. "No." He looked around and then made his way over to a wrought-iron bench. He sat down on it hard and took in another deep breath.

"You sure?" asked Evie, sitting next to him.

Sebastian nodded, not meaning it in the least. *Okay,* he told himself, *try to forget that you're skipping school for the first time ever and that it was really wrong to do that and who knows what you might be missing right now.* "I think so. I think it's another panic attack, but other than that I'm okay."

"This is about skipping school again, isn't it?" asked Evie.

Sebastian nodded.

Evie leaned back against the bench and shook her head. "Sebastian, I'm so sorry. I'm making you do all this because you've been so supportive and so helpful. But you don't really need to come if it's all too much."

For some reason hearing that just made him panic more. It was almost as if the thought of not helping her and not finding Benedict was worse than skipping school. It was a confusing moment for Sebastian, but he sat upright and said, "No, no. I want to help. I do. See, all better!" He turned to her and smiled a kind of forced grin, and Evie laughed.

"That smile is so not believable."

"But I'm being sincere." And he was; he just was also, you know, freaking out.

Evie nodded and laughed again. "Okay. Well. Thank you. Now then . . . let's see . . ." Evie pulled out the map of the university they'd printed off the Internet, and Sebastian gazed out before him, watching as a professor on a bicycle almost ran down a student on the grass. "So it said he taught in Albert College . . . ," said Evie, though it almost sounded like she was talking to herself.

Sebastian nodded. "Yeah, that way!" he said, pointing to their left at a large gray brick building topped with Gothic spires and a tall Gothic clock tower. Evie looked up from the map.

"How did you know that?" She looked quite surprised.

"Oh, uh." Sebastian felt that familiar flush of shame that always came over him at times like these.

"What, what is it?" asked Evie.

"It's just," he said, "I've got a photographic memory. I look at something and it's as if I've taken a picture of it. It's why I'm so good with math and science stuff."

"That's really impressive," said Evie. "Aren't you proud?"

Not really, thought Sebastian. "I guess I just . . ."

"What?"

"Well, it's kind of cheating, isn't it? It's not really smart, not like the way my brother and sister are smart. It's too easy."

"I don't think it's like that," she replied thoughtfully. "I think we all have our strengths and weaknesses and are lucky to have certain talents. I can sing, and it never took me a lot of work to be good at it." She stopped short, as if she had caught herself saying something she shouldn't. "Well, anyway, I think it's neat, and let's just go find Benedict now."

Sebastian nodded. Having a task to do was an excellent way to ignore all the emotions he was feeling. And he suspected Evie was using it the same way.

They stood up and made their way over to the building just as the bell in the clock tower chimed.

Sebastian actually jumped in surprise and Evie giggled at his reaction. But she stopped short as a young man racing into the building cut her off, almost taking her nose with him. Suddenly there was a large influx of students sweeping past them in a rush. The next class appeared to be starting.

"Where did they all come from?" asked Evie in amazement.

"No idea," Sebastian replied, quickly stepping to the side as a girl with two large bags in each hand and a backpack on her shoulders came barreling by.

"Okay, so the plan. Find Benedict," said Evie.

"That's always been the plan, hasn't it?"

"Just repeating it." Evie looked at her map. "I think you should go to his class and I'll go to his office. Maybe there's some information there."

"I don't think we should split up," said Sebastian. He didn't like the thought of finding and speaking with Benedict Barnes on his own. He wasn't good at improvising lies the way Evie was.

"It'll save time," replied Evie, folding up the university map. "I know where his office is, but you'll have to ask someone about his class. It's in this building, that much we know. Remember, his last name is Silo here."

Sebastian swallowed hard and stared at the tall oak

doors before him. "Why don't you go to his class? You're better at talking to people."

"Why do you think that?" she asked, looking quite surprised.

"My parents . . . last night . . . you were able to lie to them and make up stories and make small talk. It was . . . well, I guess it was kind of impressive."

Evie stared at him for a moment and Sebastian started to feel a little uncomfortable. "Thank you," she said so sincerely and so warmly, it almost made Sebastian blush. "I can't think of the last compliment someone gave me."

"Oh, well. You're welcome." He was feeling too uncomfortable now; time to change the subject. "So anyway, you'll go to the class, then?"

"No. It's a class on cartography, and with all your maps all over your bedroom and your impressive photographic memory, I think you're better suited to pretend to be a student."

"Pretend to be a student?" Sebastian was feeling that panic sensation again.

"Of course! How else will you fit in with the class?"

"Evie. I'm twelve!"

"Who cares? There are prodigies, aren't there? Kids who go to university? No one will question you, they'll be too impressed. Now get going; the crowds have thinned—class is starting soon!" Without pause, Evie walked up to the oak doors and pulled one open. Sebastian followed, and soon they were in the dark, looming foyer of the college.

"Good luck!" said Evie, and she started to climb the wide wooden staircase before them, passing a large sculpture of a fox carved into the top of the banister.

"Wait, where do I meet you after?" Sebastian called out. Evie turned and looked down at him.

"The base of the clock tower."

And with that she was running up the steps, taking them two by two.

Sebastian stared as she disappeared, and took a few moments to steady himself. Then he turned just in time to walk right into a tall man in a black leather jacket. "Oh, I . . . uh, I'm sorry," he said. He looked up and had to contain his shock at what he saw. Half of the man's face appeared to be, well, for want of a better word, *melted*. The man gave a curt nod and was about to walk off when Sebastian asked, "Do you know where Professor Silo's class is today?"

The man stared at him for a moment. For too long a moment, really. It made Sebastian feel terribly uncomfortable. "No," he said abruptly, and he marched off up the staircase.

Sebastian sighed.

"I do!" said a warm voice from behind him. Sebastian turned and there was a short, friendly-looking young woman with a mass of red curly hair smiling at him brightly.

Sebastian felt instant relief. "You do?"

"Yup! Follow me!" she said.

She led him down a dark hallway that turned into a brightly lit corridor opening onto a courtyard. They pushed through a set of doors and walked outside under a sheltered colonnade and back through another set of doors, continuing until they finally reached a large classroom set up like an amphitheater: rows of seats stacked above each other, making the room two stories tall. It was jam-packed with students.

"Thank goodness, we're on time!" said the young woman, and she darted into the room. Sebastian had no choice but to follow her. Well, he probably had many choices, and his brain acknowledged that as he rushed into the room and sat at the only other available desk beside her in the front row, but his body didn't seem aware of the other options.

The door slammed shut and Sebastian jumped, looking back toward the entrance. A tall young man with long hair in a ponytail and wearing a blazer and jeans walked to the middle of the room and dropped his leather satchel on the desk at the front.

He looked at everyone with a gleeful glint in his eye. "*Buon giorno,* class," he said, not at all pronouncing the Italian words for "good day" correctly, though he spoke it with an odd smugness. "Pop quiz!"

There were frustrated murmurs from the students behind him, and Sebastian joined them. He leaned over to the redheaded young woman and asked, "Where's Professor Silo?"

"What do you mean?"

"That's not him," said Sebastian, nodding at Mr. Ponytail.

"Right. That's Derrick."

Sebastian stared at her as she pulled a pair of pens from her purse. She looked up then, noticing his confused expression.

"The TA," she said. He continued to stare. "Teacher's assistant?" she said, now looking equally confused.

"What?" Okay, next time he was going to ask a specific question, not let surprise hold him back like this.

"Wow, you've missed a lot of classes," she said, shaking her head. "Derrick's been teaching us for over a month now."

"What? *Why?*" Nope, evidently all he could do was blurt out single questions beginning with *W.*

The young woman frowned at him and for the first

time regarded him with suspicion. "Because," she said slowly, "Professor Silo has been off photographing the Vertiginous Volcano for the last six weeks."

Evie felt quietly confident walking down the empty corridor that led to the faculty offices. They were on to something. They would find Benedict Barnes, and they would hopefully find the key, and then she'd get it to her grandfather . . . step by step, like her footsteps now, echoing along the polished marble floor.

She arrived at 18B and knocked on the door. She knew Benedict was teaching right now, but one could never be too careful, or too polite. No response. She tried the doorknob and was relieved when it turned easily and she opened the door. The room inside was very small. So small, in fact, that the door could only open halfway before it hit the desk running along the length of one wall. She slipped inside and looked around. Above the desk was a large map of ancient Rome, and opposite the desk was a bookshelf stuffed full with books. On the far wall opposite the door was a small open window above a table on which a large leather-bound atlas lay open to a map of the world. Benedict Barnes had certainly managed to cram a lot of stuff into the tiny space. She felt quite daunted by the prospect of finding a key in the crowded room with maps everywhere. If only that were what she was looking for. If one wanted to find a map, this was the place to do it. If books with titles like *The Complete Topography of Western Canada* and *Rivers, Lakes, Oceans, and Puddles of the World* weren't overwhelming enough, the desk itself was piled high with them, all scattered about in a disorganized fashion.

Evie stared at the room and decided she might as well start searching. She began by going through the drawers of the desk, but all she found were old cameras and empty film canisters. She then decided to attempt the top of the desk. Maybe a key was hidden underneath the pile of maps. It seemed daunting, but she was determined. She began to sort through the papers.

Halfway through her task she noticed an invitation buried under a map of the inside of the local television station. She picked it up and looked at who it was from, gasping at what she read: "Catherine Lind." The former animal expert of the former Filipendulous Five! Evie felt a flutter of butterflies in her stomach just as the invitation fluttered in her hand. A breeze from the open window at the end of the room swept the card from her grasp and sent it flying toward the doorway. Evie bent down to pick it up, only to see that it had landed on top of a heavy black boot.

"What are you doing?" a voice asked.

Evie snatched up the invitation and stood, her insides running cold at what she saw. Facing her, both silhouetted by the doorframe and lit by the light from the window, was the melted man. She straightened, paralyzed with fear, able to do nothing more than blink a few times. *Do something, Evie,* she told herself. *Say something. It looks more suspicious if you just stare like that.*

"Oh. Hello," she said.

The man cocked his head to the side slightly and squinted at her.

"I, uh, I wanted to talk to the professor, but he's not here, so I thought maybe I'd help him organize his papers. . . ." The words were coming out in a frantic stream as she hoped that maybe he wouldn't recognize her. Some grown-ups thought that kids all looked alike, or didn't really notice kids in the first place. Hopefully he was one of those adults.

He took a step toward her. His eyes opened wide in realization.

Or maybe not.

"Anyway, probably a bad idea, so I'm going to just go now. . . ." But of course going was pretty much impossible, as the half-open door was completely blocked by a man the size of a wall.

The melted man put his hand to his hip, pushing back his jacket and revealing a holstered old-fashioned-looking gun.

Evie's breathing got fast and inefficient, a bit like she was a dachshund attempting to dog-paddle. She took a step backward.

"You look very familiar," growled the man.

"Really? How neat," squeaked Evie.

"What's that?"

Evie squeezed the invitation tightly between her fingers.

"Nothing." She took another step backward.

"That's clearly something." And he pointed with his other hand.

Evie looked over her shoulder. "Where?" she asked, trying her best to act stupid. She stared at the atlas hard.

"Not over your shoulder, in your hand." The man's growling had become more guttural, deeper and angrier.

Evie looked at her right hand, the one that wasn't holding the invitation. She really couldn't keep up this pretending-to-be-stupid game for long.

"The other hand!" the man roared at her.

Evie took another step backward. She looked at the invitation. Something inside her told her she shouldn't let it go. "Oh. This. It's nothing. It's just—"

And then she spun around, leapt up onto the atlas, and pulled herself through the tiny window, scrambling out onto what was fortunately a sill, though unfortunately, an incredibly narrow one. The man's hands appeared through the window a moment later, grabbing at her fleeing foot. She narrowly avoided him, scrambling to hold on to the side of the building. She pulled herself up to standing and walked carefully along the wall away from the window, willing herself not to look down.

The man stuck his head out the window and stared at her, aghast. She understood the feeling; she was pretty aghast herself. What on earth had possessed her to just launch herself out through a third-story window like that? Well, fear for her life, she supposed.

The window was far too small for him to crawl through, so she turned and continued her journey, holding her body flat against the building, inching her way along its side until she made it to a drainage pipe covered in ivy. She looked up. The roof wasn't so far away, and it did look a lot safer than her tiny brick ledge. Evie turned back to the man and almost fainted. She grabbed on to the pipe tightly, just as her

feet slipped out from beneath her; then she steadied herself and stared at the gun sticking out through the window, aimed directly at her.

"Come back, girly," said the man. "I don't want to have to shoot you."

"You really shouldn't feel any obligation to, you know," she called back, pretty certain that such a reasonable suggestion would be lost on him. Sure enough, the man cocked the gun instead.

The decision was made. She turned and began to climb as quickly as she could, using the ivy as a kind of rope ladder and pulling herself up the drainage pipe.

There was a loud explosion from behind her as the

man fired his gun, but Evie didn't look back. She just let her adrenaline take her upward at an impressive speed until she was at the roof, pulling herself up by her hands and rolling onto the flat surface. A wave of relief washed over her.

Evie sat up quickly and looked around. There was a fire exit down at the other end of the roof by one of the Gothic towers. She got to her feet and made her way over to it, suddenly feeling the ache in her muscles and the hitch in her lungs. She was also realizing just what a dangerous thing she'd done, and fear coursed through her veins as she reached for the door handle. Fortune was on her side again; it too was unlocked. She yanked the door open.

And then fortune decided to switch teams.

The melted man was right there below, rushing up the stairs to get her. She slammed the door shut and ran in the opposite direction, looking around frantically as she did. And then she saw it.

The clock tower.

>CHAPTER 13<

In which we experience a higher education. Literally and figuratively.

"Oh. Well, in that case, I have to go." Sebastian stood up, but was yanked fiercely down back into his seat by the redheaded young woman. "Ow!" he said, staring at her with confusion.

"You can't leave now, you'll fail the class!" she whispered.

"But that doesn't matter to me," replied Sebastian, starting to feel more than a little trapped. What good was staying here when Benedict Barnes wasn't around? It would make so much more sense for him to find Evie at the office and help her search for the key. He stood up again.

"Now," said Derrick the TA with a grin, "I thought

we might have a bit of fun with this quiz and do it game-show-style. Be a little competitive and a little theatrical and—where exactly do you think you're going?"

Sebastian was slowly making his way down the front of the first row of seats. He was working so hard to be as quiet and unnoticeable as possible that he didn't realize that Derrick the TA was speaking to him. It was only when the silence grew ominous and he could hear the clock on the wall ticking with existential angst that he looked up and realized everyone was staring at him.

"Sorry, what was the question?" he asked.

"*Dio mio,*" said Derrick the TA in frustration, once again completely butchering the Italian. "Where are you going?"

"Uh . . . I'm leaving." Why couldn't he just go? This was grown-up school, after all; weren't grown-ups allowed to do what they wanted, leave places if they so desired?

"I'm afraid I can't let you do that," replied Derrick the TA, crossing his arms over his chest.

And that was when Sebastian realized something amazing. He *couldn't* get in trouble. He wasn't a student here. But it also wasn't illegal to sit and observe a class (he knew that because his sister used to do that for fun when she was a teenager). And he wanted to leave. So that was what he was going to do.

With a great deal of confidence, Sebastian ignored Derrick the TA and went to the door. Now, if he'd been having the same kind of luck as Evie had been up until a few moments earlier, it would have been unlocked and he would have left and that would have been that. But he wasn't.

"Yes. The door's locked," said Derrick the TA, and he gave a low guttural laugh that sounded far too evil for the situation.

"I need to go. It's . . . an emergency!" said Sebastian, and it was indeed starting to feel like one.

"Do you have a doctor's note?"

"No."

"Then it's not an emergency."

Sebastian was pretty annoyed now. This was ridiculous, and he did not have a proper appreciation for the ridiculous or the absurd. "Well, what can I say to convince you to let me leave?"

Derrick the TA stroked the peach fuzz of a beard on his chin and then looked at Sebastian with another inappropriately evil smile. "You get a perfect score on the quiz, I'll let you leave class early."

Now, normally, taking a quiz without having studied for it would have filled Sebastian with a sense of dread. Fear, even. But in that moment Sebastian was feeling pretty darn annoyed with Derrick the TA, and that smug, stupid smile of his had sufficiently worked its way under Sebastian's skin. On top of all that, this was a class about maps and geography, and if there was one thing Sebastian's excellent photographic memory had consumed lots of, it was that.

"Yeah, okay. Let's do this." He walked up to Derrick the TA and put his hands on his hips. "Is this a team thing or, like, a spelling bee or what?"

"Hmm . . . I think for you I have a special kind of quiz. Everyone in the class gets to ask you a question. You miss one, you have to sit it out for the rest of the class."

Sebastian stared at Derrick the TA in disbelief. "Why are you acting like a comic-book villain?"

"Because this is the only time I have any power over anyone in my life. So, are you going to play the game or not?"

Sebastian stared out at the vast classroom before him. There had to be at least a hundred students staring back. Well, it wasn't like he had a choice.

"Let's play," he said.

Evie raced to the clock tower and felt very much that normal racing in gym class had left her woefully ill prepared for this moment. Never before had she raced while consumed by such a sense of panic, not to mention the whole adrenaline and staring-death-in-the-face part. She focused on this life-and-death balance as she ran across the roof, avoiding chimney tops and a remarkable number of weather vanes.

The melted man was far enough behind her that she was able to make some decisions as she ran, but there was really only one way to the clock tower, and that was the way she intended to go. She finally skidded to a stop at its base and discovered a small wooden door on its east side. She opened it and found herself staring in at the landing of a giant wooden staircase leading to a trapdoor high above. Evie had really hoped that the tower went down instead of up; she was getting tired of all this heights nonsense. But up it was and up she went.

She was almost at the trapdoor at the very top when the door far below swung open with a bang. Quickly she pushed open the hatch and a short rope ladder unfurled before her. She climbed up and made her way through the opening, pulling the ladder up once she had, and let the trapdoor fall shut behind her. She looked around for something to keep it closed.

"Whoa."

She was standing inside the clock part of the tower

itself, surrounded by four giant walls, each with an enormous translucent white clock face covered in gears and winches clicking and spinning. But what impressed her even more was the bell—it was twice as tall as a person and nearly twice as wide, and was hanging in the middle of the room. A long rope dangled from the clapper and spooled in a thick heavy coil directly beneath it, and Evie was tempted in that moment to ring the bell, just to see what it was like.

No, she didn't have time for this. Instead she ran to the coil and pushed at it. It was really heavy. So she uncoiled the rope as fast as she could and dragged it over to the trapdoor. The bell clanged loudly once as she did, startling her and causing her to stop for a moment. Bells were loud, yes, but bells right above you? Deafening. She shook her head as if shaking water out of her ears and then continued with the task at hand. Eventually Evie managed to coil the rope on top of the trapdoor. She stared at it for a moment, panting. Good. That would hold the melted man off for a little bit, at any rate.

Now for a way to get out of there.

Sebastian hated to admit it, but he was having fun. He was also enjoying wiping the smug look off Derrick the

TA's face as he answered every single question posed to him correctly. The game had started off slow; no one in the class seemed really all that interested in playing. But as Sebastian began to answer question after question, the energy in the room had shifted, students leaned forward in their seats, and even the guy carving something into his desk in the back row glanced up with slight interest.

"How long is the Great Wall of China?"

"Five thousand five hundred miles or eight thousand eight hundred and fifty-two kilometers."

"Who is the earliest ancient Greek to have created a map of the world?"

"Anaximander."

"What's the longest street in the world?"

"Yonge Street."

It was only when Sebastian heard the clock tower clang once, even though it was now past one o'clock, that he was jarred back to the reality of the situation. *Evie*. He'd forgotten all about her! And he was supposed to meet her at the tower.

"Hey, Derrick," said Sebastian, "this is taking too much time. Any way we can speed this up? I mean, I've been answering everything really easily. Can't we just say I'm the winner?"

"That's not how the game is played," replied Derrick the TA through clenched teeth.

"But you just made up the game right now. Surely the rules—"

"The rules are whatever I make them!" he bellowed back, and everyone in the class sat in stunned silence.

"Okay, Derrick, seriously, chill," said the redheaded young woman in the front row.

"I will not chill! I will not chill and be made a mockery of by this extremely young-looking college-aged student! I am a postgrad. A *post*grad! I am older, and wiser, and am working on my PhD, for crying out loud! My *P. H. D*! I demand respect!"

"Respect isn't demanded, it's earned," said Sebastian quietly.

"Shut up!" Derrick the TA's face was nearly the color of the redheaded young woman's hair now.

"How about this," said the redheaded young woman in a tone one would use to calm a toddler. "You ask one final question. If he gets it right, he gets to go. If he gets it wrong, he sits down. Just like your rules dictated."

Derrick the TA thought about it for a moment and then gave a curt nod.

"Fine. One last question." He walked slowly toward Sebastian, seething with every step. "What country am I thinking of right now?"

Sebastian stared at him. "What kind of a question is that?" he asked, completely at a loss.

"Not fair!" called out a voice from the far back of the room.

"It's perfectly fair!" snapped Derrick the TA. He turned back to look at Sebastian with that grin of his. "Go on."

There was no logical way to answer the question. There wasn't. He continued to stare at Derrick the TA. This was impossible. Sebastian racked his brain for something, anything. He thought back to the TA's odd greeting at the beginning of class. The poorly pronounced words . . . It was a guess, that's all it was. But it seemed an educated one, at the very least.

"Italy?" said Sebastian.

What little color Derrick the TA had in his face drained out of it completely. "That's—that's—" he stammered.

"Yes?" asked Sebastian.

"That's correct."

"Yes!" The red-haired young woman sprang to her feet, punching the air above her head with both her fists. The rest of the class burst into applause and several of them even cheered. Sebastian grinned and took in the moment, imagining this was what it was like to win at the International Mathematical Olympiad.

He turned in triumph back to Derrick the TA. "Now," he said, "will you please unlock the door?"

On stiff legs, Derrick the TA forced himself to the door. He unlocked it and threw it wide open.

"Get out!" he roared. And the class fell silent at his outburst. He looked at them and then at Sebastian. "Get out, and never come back. You've been kicked out of this class for all time!"

"Okay," said Sebastian, and he ran out of there as fast as he could.

Thud.

Evie spun around and stared at the trapdoor.

Thud.

The rope was holding it down, but the man with the melted face was definitely pushing hard to open it. She looked around the room in a panic. There was no other way out. There was only . . . down.

She ran over to the large clock face on the south side and inspected it closely. The round clock was framed by a large square made up of many individual panes of glass. Surely one had to open, for cleaning purposes at the very least. Evie made her way systematically, testing each windowpane on the south-facing clock. Then the east. Then the north. Finally, when she tried the west, one panel gave a bit under her hands.

"I knew it! They do open . . . ," she said just as she pushed harder and the entire pane fell out of the window frame and onto the grass lawn below, breaking into several pieces. "Or maybe not."

Well, whatever, at least she had an escape. Now the only question was, how to do it? She looked back into the room for an answer.

"Evie!" She heard the cry from far away. She turned and poked her head out the window.

"Sebastian, where are you?" she called out.

"At the tower. Where are you?" His voice was a little muffled but it was so comforting to hear it.

"In the tower! I'm up in the clock. I'm on the west side! Hurry!"

She watched anxiously and then Sebastian appeared from around the corner. Evie couldn't think of the last time she'd been so happy to see someone. She waved.

"How did you get up there?" he asked, clearly astonished.

"I was chased. He's still chasing me. I need to get down!"

Thud. Evie whipped around. She waited a moment, and then the man pushed the door open, much wider this time, the boards on either side of the door cracking and splintering, and then the door slammed shut.

"Let me get help!" said Sebastian.

"There's no time, he's breaking in. I need to get down! How do I do it?" She was really beginning to feel frantic.

Sebastian stared up at her, mouth agape. He shook his head and rubbed his hands together in a panic. "I don't know! Do you have a rope?"

"Of course I don't have a rope, if I had a rope I'd—" Evie stopped. She turned around slowly and stared at the coiled rope attached to the giant bell. It was an idea. A very risky and dangerous and life-threatening idea.

"I have a rope!" she called down to Sebastian.

"Great, okay. So I guess, use it?" Sebastian sounded less sure than she felt, which did not give her much confidence.

"I don't know . . . ," she said.

"You can do it!" he called up to her, sounding a bit more believable this time.

Easy for you to say, safe on the ground like that. She looked back at the rope. She had no idea how long it would wind up being, if it would even take her to the ground. She sighed. What choice did she have?

"Okay, I'm going for it," she called down. Sebastian gave her a thumbs-up, and she nodded. Then she pulled herself back into the clock tower room and approached the rope. She needed to do this all in one quick movement or the melted man would get her. She had one chance.

This wasn't remotely terrifying.

She approached the rope and grabbed the end. It was so thick she couldn't get her fingers all the way around it. She really hoped she'd be able to hold on. *One,* she counted to herself. *Two . . . Here goes nothing. . . . Three!*

She pulled the rope as hard as she could and ran toward the window. Behind her she could hear the trapdoor crash open and the sound of grunting as the melted man pulled himself into the room. Evie flung herself at the window and dove through it like she was diving into a lake, holding fast to the rope.

Then she was outside, falling, the air rushing fast past her body. She held on tightly as she watched the green grass fly upward toward her. Suddenly she was yanked upright again and the bell let off an enormous peal. She was, quite literally, at the end of her rope.

Evie found herself flying toward the tower wall in a blur. She stuck her feet out to protect herself and bounced off the wall. Then she was swinging back, a little slower, and the bell chimed again. She dangled, still slightly swinging side to side, staring wide-eyed at Sebastian.

"Evie! Jump!" he cried. He sounded terrified. Evie

glanced up, and sure enough, the melted man was looking out the window at her. The rope suddenly quivered as he grabbed it. She looked down in horror.

She wasn't so far from the ground, maybe only one story up. She could jump; she could do it.

The rope quivered again, this time more violently. Evie looked up and saw the melted man climbing out onto the rope himself. Really? He couldn't use the stairs?

Once again time was of the essence, and just to drive home the point, the large hand on the clock above her ticked loudly, moving ahead one notch.

"Please, Evie!" called Sebastian. "Jump! I'll catch you!"

Considering he was no bigger than she was, the offer was small comfort. But it didn't matter; she really only had one option.

She took a deep breath.

And jumped.

Sebastian was flat on his back, his neck twisted at an awkward angle. "You okay?" he asked into Evie's hair.

"I think so." Evie pushed herself off and looked down at him. "Are you?"

"Not sure," replied Sebastian. He sat up and

cracked his neck. Evie made a face. "That's better. Sorry I didn't catch you."

"Well, I mean, you sort of did," she replied with a smile. She glanced upward. "We'd better run. That guy is relentless." Sebastian followed Evie's gaze; the man was halfway down the rope already.

They scrambled to their feet and pushed their way through the group of students that had gathered around them. Once free, they started to run.

"So, did you find out anything?" asked Evie as they ran past some students playing Frisbee.

"No. Well, yes," replied Sebastian. "He's not here. He's not in the country. He's off photographing the Vertiginous Volcano."

"Oh," said Evie, sounding disappointed, and Sebastian could understand her feeling. Not only was it too bad that Benedict wasn't here to help them, it also meant that she had risked her life for nothing. "That's really a shame."

"Yeah." They finally made it to the gates of the university and flew through them and out onto the city street. They continued to run, even though by now they were pretty sure they weren't being chased, until finally they ducked down an alley next to the bus station and hid behind a large garbage dumpster.

"Well," said Evie, panting slightly, "there is some

good news. I found this invitation." She passed it over to Sebastian and he had a look.

"It's from Catherine Lind!" So it looked like at least two of the team members were still in touch with each other. And one of them at least had kept her real name. That was interesting.

Evie nodded. "It's for a talk she's giving."

"Yeah," he said as he read it. "Tonight."

"I think we should go. We couldn't find Benedict, but maybe Catherine can help."

He handed back the invitation and looked at her. She had a sparkle in her eye. Sebastian couldn't believe it. Despite everything she'd just gone through, it seemed she still wanted to press on. "Do you really want to do this? It would appear we aren't the only ones looking for the key. If that man was there looking for Benedict just like we were, chances are he'll be looking for Catherine, too."

"I know. I know that. But I have to do this. And anyway, the man didn't see the invitation, so maybe he doesn't know about the talk!" She sounded so hopeful that Sebastian almost believed she could be right. Almost.

"Okay, but we need to ask my parents' permission to go," said Sebastian, grateful he wouldn't have to lie to them. Not really.

"Sure! I mean, it's an educational talk. I imagine they are supportive of those. Anything to further your studies." Evie grinned from ear to ear.

"They are." It was true. They'd probably let him eat candy for breakfast if he told them it was for an experiment for school. Not that he wanted to do that, of course. That wasn't a healthy way to start the morning.

Evie leaned against the dumpster and exhaled slowly. "Well. That was eventful. Hey, wait—if Benedict wasn't in the class, what did you get up to that whole time?"

"Oh, it's really not worth talking about. It was very silly."

"Fair enough," said Evie, peeking around the dumpster. "Should we head back to your place?"

"Yeah. Let's go."

"And we'll get ready for phase two!" said Evie with a grin.

"Yeah," said Sebastian, smiling back in an attempt to show solidarity but just feeling exhausted and scared. "Phase two."

➤ CHAPTER 14 ◄

In which we don't attend a lecture.

Sure enough, it was relatively easy to get permission from Sebastian's parents for them to go to Catherine's lecture that night. They were all for it, and even suggested they come along too. But Sebastian had made it clear that he wanted to go on his own, and his parents were quite respectful of that request and dropped him and Evie off without lingering, taking only the briefest of moments to let them know they'd be back in two hours to pick them up. Evie had felt a pang in her gut, watching the three of them interact. How she longed for something similar. To have such support and trust. From someone.

Now, I'm not sure how many lecture halls you've

been in,[10] but to say the lecture hall in which the world-famous explorer and animal activist Catherine Lind was to present that evening was underwhelming would be like saying getting socks on your birthday is underwhelming. It was so terribly underwhelming, you could have called it under-underwhelming.

The lecture was in the basement of a community center on the outskirts of town. A dozen chairs had been set up before a music stand, and as Evie and Sebastian sat down in the back row, which was also the second row, Evie was pretty offended on behalf of Catherine Lind.

Sebastian appeared to feel the same. "This isn't right," he whispered to her, though they were actually alone. "She should be talking on the main stage of the Royal Theatre, not here. I really wish we knew what happened to the team. They were so famous once, and now she's talking in a place like this. It's so . . . odd."

"I agree," replied Evie.

They waited patiently until seven more seats were filled. And then finally a little hunched man began the journey from a small door at the back of the room toward the music stand. There was silence as the audi-

---

[10] I have been in twenty-three.

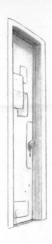

ence watched him cross the room at a snail's pace.[11] He finally arrived at the stand, and at a similarly intolerable pace he began to push down the top of the stand so that it collapsed into itself inch by inch. It made a high-pitched squeal that caused Evie's entire body to tense up. Then, when it was no longer than the length of a cane, he picked it up, turned around, and began the arduous journey back to the door. And then he was gone.

"What . . . what just happened?" asked Evie, turning to look at Sebastian.

"I don't know," he replied. He looked just as confused as Evie felt.

The audience members got up and began shuffling toward the exit.

---

[11] Though it was even slower than that and a bit of an insult to snails.

"Excuse me, ma'am," said Evie to a passing woman wearing a bright red coat made entirely of fringe. "Why are you leaving?"

"The lecture has been canceled," replied the woman with a sigh, and then continued on her way.

"No," Sebastian said as Evie watched the woman leave. "That can't be. Why?"

In a flash, Evie was up on her feet and heading to the small door through which the old man had disappeared.

"This isn't a good idea," she heard from behind her, but Sebastian was following her nonetheless.

She pushed open the door at the back of the room and walked right into what turned out to be a very messy office. The old man was pushing around some pieces of paper on a desk in what looked like an attempt to tidy it, but really he just sort of shifted the paper around into different and unique patterns.

"Sir," said Evie as politely as she could manage, "do you know where Catherine Lind is?"

The man began turning his head, and Evie waited impatiently for him to look at her.

He finally did and blinked at her once, then again, from behind a pair of thick round glasses. He opened his mouth and licked his lips and then, eventually, said, "Yes."

"Yes!" Evie was surprised at the answer. But it was good to hear. "And where is she?"

The old man looked down and then looked up. Then he very slowly scratched the top of his right ear. Then he blinked. Then he said, "The zoo."

"The zoo? Are you sure?" asked Sebastian, taking a step so he was standing beside Evie.

"Well . . . ," said the old man. Then he squinted as if thinking hard. Then he closed his eyes. Then he started to snore.

"Sir?" said Evie. She looked at Sebastian, who shrugged back at her. She said it again a little louder. "Sir?"

The old man jolted awake and stared at her, seeming totally confused about what she wanted from him.

"Catherine Lind is at the zoo," said Evie, trying to remind him of their very recent conversation. "My friend asked you if you were sure because it's nighttime and normally the zoo is closed at this time. How do you know she's at the zoo?" Evie found that in her effort to communicate with him, her words were starting to come out slowly as well.

The man nodded three times and then said, "She was invited five days ago. Sick lizard. She has not been back here or home." He paused for too long a moment. Then he pointed to the desk. Evie looked at Sebastian and he went over to the desk.

"Piles of mail . . . ," said Sebastian. Evie watched as Sebastian riffled through the mountain of paper all the way down to the wood of the desk and grabbed a letter. He examined it and, looking at Evie, said, "Five days old." He turned back to the old man. "Did you tell anyone? Have you been investigating her absence in any way?"

The old man exhaled slowly. He looked up at the ceiling, thinking long and hard. Then he looked back at Sebastian and nodded thoughtfully. "Was getting round to it."

"Let's go," said Sebastian. Evie nodded.

"Thank you for your help!" Evie called as they rushed out of the room.

"You're wel—"

They closed the door behind them and made their way across the basement, past the chairs, up the staircase, and finally out the front door of the center and into the deserted parking lot.

"So what do you think?" asked Sebastian.

"I think if the old man is right, then something suspicious is going on. I think Catherine is still at the zoo. And if she is, she's in serious trouble." Evie was starting to feel frightened again. She thought back to the university. At the time it had simply seemed fortunate that only one of the men had been there to chase them. Now she feared it was not fortune at all, but something far more sinister. The other man had been keeping watch over Catherine. "We should go to the zoo tomorrow, to find out for sure," she said, trying to come across as brave and not terrified.

Sebastian nodded. He, on the other hand, didn't look nearly as confident as she was pretending to be.

Once again, she felt pretty bad for the guy. "It's okay, Sebastian, you don't have to—"

"You need to stop saying that," said Sebastian with a tight smile. "You know I'm going to help you. I might not have the constitution for adventures, but I still want to do this. I'm in it now and I need to see this through to the end. No convincing needed."

"Okay. Thanks. Again. And hey, at least tomorrow's Saturday. You won't have to skip school," said Evie, trying to find the bright side.

"Small miracles," replied Sebastian. He looked like he might throw up.

"Small miracles," she said.

Though, man, she could really do with a big one.

CHAPTER 15

In which we visit a creepy zoo.

After a much-needed sleep, Sebastian and Evie were ready in the morning for their next adventure. Sebastian was surprised how stiff and sore he felt; he had not ever considered the physical ramifications of adventuring. And as they made their way once again through the city by bus, he realized he also hadn't considered just how costly it was either. Bus fares did add up after a while.

The zoo had once housed some of the most exotic and rare animals that roamed the earth, or swam the seas, or flew the skies, or just kind of sat there blinking at you. In its glory days it had been a bustling place, filled with locals and tourists alike. Sebastian could only vaguely remember that time. But things change, and people began to realize that the cages for the animals seemed a little cramped, and the staff of the zoo not nearly large enough to take care of all the beasts properly. Some people thought this was wrong and began to say so, and eventually petitions were signed, and bit by bit various animals were taken away from the zoo to larger, more appropriate animal reserves. Though Sebastian and Evie didn't know it then, Catherine herself had been one of the main crusaders of the movement to relocate the animals.

The few animals that had stayed at the zoo were nice in their way, but far less exotic than those that had been moved, and because it wasn't nearly as exciting as it once had been, people began avoiding the zoo, and now the formerly fine institution had become almost deserted.

So it was that when Sebastian and Evie arrived the next morning, the place was far from welcoming. The wrought-iron gates were unlocked, but a chain still dangled from one, and while Sebastian supposed it was meant to indicate that the zoo was open for business, it looked more like an accident that the doors were open, as if people weren't really supposed to step inside. Sebastian looked at Evie, hesitant to enter, but she was already walking through the gates, stepping through the wet dead leaves covering the ground.

The once-friendly cobblestone streets were cracked, and there were stagnant puddles where bricks were missing. Cages were empty and overgrown, the names of their former inhabitants eclipsed by dead over-

growth. It was an eerily quiet place. The absence of crowds and animal sounds made the quiet all the more palpable. *There should be life here,* thought Sebastian, a shiver passing over him. This was where you came to experience all kinds of living creatures. And now it seemed as if practically everything was dead.

"This isn't creepy at all," said Evie.

"You don't think so? I find it all very unsettling," replied Sebastian, stopping before a large faded map of the zoo. So faded, in fact, that all he could see was the little red dot with YOU ARE HERE written on it. You are here, floating in the middle of a large white space. You are nowhere.

"Uh, I wasn't being serious. This place is seriously creepy. I can't understand why the zoo hasn't been shut down completely. Why they have any animals at all."

Sebastian nodded. It was true—it didn't really make much sense. None of it did. Even the fact that he was here in the first place. What was it about the Filipendulous Five that made him take so many risks? It freaked him out. He stared at the sign. A red dot. Like a red warning light. *You shouldn't be here.*

"Okay, so should we split up, then?" asked Evie.

"No. No, we shouldn't. Don't you remember what happened last time?" replied Sebastian, shocked she would even think of such a thing after their experience the day before.

"But it'll take longer if we don't."

Sebastian was adamant. "It'll take even longer if one of us goes missing. No risks."

"Well, not *no* risks. Some risks. Carefully calculated risks," replied Evie.

You shouldn't be here.

"Okay, fine. Carefully calculated risks. But that's it." Sebastian didn't even really like the thought of a careful risk, but the fact was he was already taking a big one being here in the first place, so he couldn't really disagree with her. He could feel his breath grow shallow once more at the thought, and he told himself it was just for today. That was all. Just today. Hopefully they'd find Catherine Lind, they'd find out where the key was, they'd figure out where Evie's grandfather was, and then, tomorrow, Sebastian would be back to his regular routine.

The thought calmed him considerably.

"So, a sick lizard. I guess we should start at the Reptile Realm?" asked Sebastian.

"I think that makes the most sense," agreed Evie.

The two of them made their way farther into the depths of the zoo. It was a good thing that Sebastian had his excellent memory from when he'd visited the zoo years ago, because so much of the place was like a maze. Finding the Reptile Realm could have been tricky if not for his remembering the path he'd once taken as a small child to find it.

"It really seems deserted," commented Evie.

"Yeah."

"Sad."

Sebastian wasn't sure why exactly it was a sad thing that there weren't people around. There weren't many animals to look at except the llamas they'd just passed, who'd chewed at them as they went by. Why would people be here? Wouldn't the people be more sad and disappointed to come to a zoo with so few animals?

"There it is," said Sebastian, pointing, and before he could feel any sense of pride at having brought them to the spot so successfully, he was suddenly pulled off the path and down into the brush and mud next to it. "What was that for?" he asked, staring at Evie.

"Shh!" she ordered, a finger to her lips as she pointed behind him. Sebastian peeked out through the plants and saw a man in a black leather jacket step out of a small side entrance to the Reptile Realm. There was a sign over the door that said STAFF ONLY. It was hard to tell exactly what was wrong with his face, but it kind of looked as if half of it was melted off, including his ear. They watched as he carefully locked the door behind him and pocketed the key.

"Wait, I recognize that zookeeper," Sebastian whispered, his mind racing back to the man he'd run into at the university.

"That's no zookeeper," Evie whispered back, a slight tremble to her voice. "He's the man who chased me into the clock tower and burned down the Andersons' house."

"Well, he could be a zookeeper also," pointed out Sebastian, though even as he said it, he knew it was beside the point.

Evie shook her head. "It doesn't matter what his job is; the point is this means we were right—Catherine is probably in real trouble."

"So what should we do?"

"We have to find out if Catherine is even in there with the reptiles and what's going on," replied Evie. She sounded very sure of herself. "If we can get a look in through the main doors of the Reptile Realm and assess the situation, then we can make a real plan."

Sebastian considered it and did agree that what she was suggesting was one of those well-calculated risks.

"Then let's do it," he said, and turned to look at her. "What?" She was looking back at him with one of her unreadable expressions.

"Uh, I think . . ." She stopped talking.

"Just say it," he said, a growing sense of unease filling his body.

Evie sighed. She did that a lot. "Okay. I think you should be the one to go look and I should stay hidden."

Sebastian stared at her, feeling a sudden wash of fear flood over him. "Oh."

"I know, it's not fair. You're helping *me*—it should be me taking the risks. But . . . they know who I am. If you go and look you'll be just some boy at the zoo."

"B-but . . . ," stuttered Sebastian.

"What?" asked Evie.

"I met him yesterday. For a moment. He might remember me, too." Panic was rising up inside him.

" 'Might' is better than 'will,' " replied Evie.

"Is it?" Sebastian's voice was louder and higher in pitch than he'd expected, and he glanced at the melted man. The man didn't seem to have heard him.

"Yes. Or—I don't know. I don't know what else to do! We can't just hide here forever." She looked at him with a desperate expression. "Do you think you can do this?"

Sebastian was pretty sure he had no thinking left on the subject. Just adrenaline coursing through his veins and a whooshing sound in his ears. He stared at Evie and took in a deep breath. He nodded. Yes. Yes, he could do it. Further, he realized, buried deep within the panic was a small sense of excitement. He actually *wanted* to do it. Quietly, he pried himself out of the brush and stood up. He took a deep breath and then walked as calmly as he could pretend around the corner toward the front entrance of the Reptile Realm.

"Kid! Where do you think you're going?" said a loud voice, and Sebastian turned to see the melted man striding toward him, hand on hip. Or no, rather, hand on holster, and Sebastian assumed that within the holster was some kind of gun or weapon. Sebastian swallowed. Or attempted to. Suddenly the inside of his mouth was very dry.

"Oh hi!" he said—well, kind of squeaked, actually. "I just wanted to see the lizards."

The melted man loomed over him and Sebastian attempted to swallow again. Did he recognize him? Did he remember? Was this man the last person Sebastian was ever going to see on this earth? "Exhibit's closed, kid," said the man.

Sebastian was both relieved and terrified, but he couldn't exactly turn away. He needed to see inside, to see if Catherine was there. He would have to do something unthinkable. He'd have to ignore an authority figure. He could feel his whole body shaking at the thought. "Really? I thought I saw someone inside." His throat was so dry he was barely able to get the words out, and Sebastian turned and marched on trembling legs toward the glass front doors and opened one. Suddenly his feet were no longer touching the ground. The man had grabbed him under the armpits and turned him around to face him.

"I said it's closed."

"I don't care!" said Sebastian defiantly, finding his voice. But he did care, he really did. "I think you're lying and someone's in there!"

"Oh, someone's in there, all right." The man squinted at him and Sebastian squinted back. "You want to see what happens to people who don't follow the rules and sneak into dangerous reptile exhibits? Fine!"

The man carried Sebastian over to the doors and through them. Sebastian didn't even struggle; he was paralyzed with fear. It took a moment for his eyes to adjust to the dark as he was swept quickly down the main hallway, past empty terrarium after empty terrarium, each filled with decaying tree branches, or browning grass, or old bits of newspaper from several years ago. The fluorescent lights down the hall flickered, creating an eerie stop-motion effect as they made their way down to the end of the hall, where a second

man was pacing back and forth in front of the largest
terrarium in the exhibit. The man stopped and stared
in utter confusion as they approached, and Sebastian
was certain he was staring back exactly the same way,
stunned at what he was seeing. The man's jaw was
apparently wired shut, with bits of wire poking out
through pale and cracked lips, and one even through
the flesh of his cheek. The effect was completely horrific, but Sebastian in his pragmatic way could think
only one thing: how does he eat?

"Just showing the kid what happens when you dis-
obey grown-ups," said the melted man, and the wired-

jaw man gave a nod and moved to the side, revealing the terrarium behind him.

Sebastian stared wide-eyed. There, sitting in the center of the glass enclosure, was Catherine. But she was hardly visible; only the top of her blunt red bob, forehead, and eyes could be seen. The rest of her body was hidden by a large Burmese python that had coiled its bright-yellow-and-brown-spotted body all the way around her and was now staring at them with unblinking eyes. It looked like a strange statue. How still and steady both of them were sitting. But it filled Sebastian with such a rush of horror and fear that he yelled out "Catherine!" before he could think.

"What was that?" asked the melted man, once more turning Sebastian to face him.

"Uh . . . ," said Sebastian, desperately trying to come up with an excuse for why he had just blurted out her name like that. But his mind let him down for maybe the first time in his life, and he just sort of stared at the man with a sad expression on his face.

"Who are you?" demanded the man.

"I'm no one," replied Sebastian. "Just a boy wanting to see the snakes."

"How do you know her name?" asked the man.

Once again Sebastian found he had nothing to say.

"Are you alone?" asked the man.

"Yes," said Sebastian.

"I don't believe you." The melted man turned to the wired-jaw man and said, "Search outside! I'll join you once I deal with him." The man nodded and walked by Sebastian, pulling out an old-fashioned-looking gun at his hip.

"Meanwhile," the man continued, "I think I'll let you take some time to consider whether or not telling me the truth is a good idea." The man carried Sebastian down the hall to a small door, pulled a key out of his pocket, and unlocked it. He threw Sebastian inside the room and slammed the door behind him.

Sebastian ran to the latch and tried it, but obviously it was locked. He felt panic rise inside him and tried to slow his breathing to calm himself down. Evie! He really hoped she had found a better hiding spot.

A strange muffled sound came from behind him and Sebastian turned. He realized then where he was. He was on the inside of the terrarium he had just been looking into. Staring at him were two sets of eyes: one human, the other python. The muffled sound was Catherine; she was trying to say something to him. Sebastian didn't know what to do. He knew how strong pythons were, and that they were able to crush a human easily. He couldn't exactly pry the python off her. Also he wasn't exactly that keen on getting too close to that snake mouth, thank you very much. They might not have fangs, but once a python got ahold of you with its teeth, it wasn't letting go until it was digesting you.

"What can I do? How can I help you?" asked Sebastian, desperate to do *some*thing.

Catherine tried to speak again. Then she sighed hard. She moved her body about within the python and the snake looked at her, almost, it seemed, with curiosity. Then it appeared to relax its body somewhat and Catherine was able to pull one of her arms out of the coil and push the top of the snake down.

"Finally!" she said. She looked at the snake. "I need you to pay closer attention, okay?"

The snake stared at her and Sebastian could swear it almost looked ashamed. Then it flicked its long tongue out of its mouth and quickly touched the tip of Catherine's nose. "Oh, don't try to be all cute now," replied Catherine. The snake did it again. "Yes, yes, I forgive you." The snake stopped its flicking and returned to looking at Sebastian.

"What I was trying to say," Catherine said, turning her attention to him as well, "is who the heck are you?"

➤CHAPTER 16◄

In which Evie is quite impressive.

Something had happened, Evie was sure of it. He'd been caught. That was all there was to it. Stupid, stupid Evie, thinking Sebastian would be safer than she would be. And now she'd just thrown him into the lion's den. Or . . . Reptile Realm . . . or whatever. Well, no more letting others take the risk. Now she not only had to save Catherine but Sebastian as well, and she was going to do it. She took a quick look around and then crawled out from the dirt and bushes and stood, brushing herself off. With a nod to reassure herself of her bravery, Evie marched her way over to the front doors of the Reptile Realm.

Just as the wired-jaw man came barging out of them.

He stopped.

Evie stopped.

They stared at each other. It seemed he was just as surprised to see her as she was to see him.

"Hi," said Evie.

The man stared at her.

"I, uh, I just wanted to visit the . . . reptiles. . . ." Even though the last time she'd tested her theory about whether an adult would recognize a kid it had totally backfired, Evie felt compelled to try it out again. Or it was more like she couldn't think of anything else to do.

The wired-jaw man raised his gun and aimed it at her.

Okay, so adults really did remember what kids looked like. Good to know.

Evie had no idea if he intended to shoot her, but before he could make any such decision, the melted man appeared at his side, and he too took a moment to stop and stare.

"You," he said.

"Yes, me," replied Evie. Once again she found herself playing dumb to stall for time.

"That boy," he said, "he's a friend of yours." It wasn't a question.

"Uh." She had no answer. Think of a clever lie, Evie, quick!

The melted man took a step toward her. "I think it might be time to lock you up with them and find out exactly what's going on here. Why you just happen to be every place we are. Such a coincidence."

Locked up. Well, that was good. At least they were still alive. That was very good. The man took another step toward her.

There was only one thing left to do.

Time to run.

Evie spun on her heel and sped in the opposite direction of the Reptile Realm. She turned to look, and sure enough, the two men were racing after her. She noticed the wired-jaw man had actually put his gun away. That was interesting. They clearly wanted to keep her alive. For now.

Oh, good.

She ran and ran and took a sharp right turn, trying to throw them off, and found herself in front of what had once been the bear pit enclosure. It was far below her, around thirty feet down. Some straw, dirt, and muddy water and large rocks were all that were left inside. Next to the pit was the fenced-in flat green space for the llamas. It stretched across to the other path on the far side, where the petting zoo was located. The fence right where Evie was standing, though, was too tall to climb. Evie considered continuing running along the path when she noticed that the low wall that encircled the pit preventing onlookers from falling into it curved inward away from the path. It would take her off the path and past the tall fence to the open llama field.

Evie glanced back. The men had turned the corner and were nearing her fast, so she climbed up onto the low wall. This was going to be all about not looking down into the pit. The bears might have all been transferred somewhere else, but falling into any pit would very likely result in a broken limb or two at the least. And in the case of this pit, it would leave her broken *and* trapped—easy prey for two scary men.

Small step by small step she began to inch her way along the wall as the men approached. She needed to get to the part where the wall turned away from the main path so that they couldn't just pluck her off the ledge and take her. They were almost there. *Fine,* she thought, *fine. I'll just . . . I'll run.*

And Evie ran, her arms outstretched to maintain balance. She turned her head slightly, and out of the corner of her eye she could see the wired-jaw man getting close, reaching his hand toward her. She picked up her speed, teetering dangerously on the wall. There was the curve! She ran faster. And faster. Wired-jaw man kept reaching, and Evie held her breath and leapt, flying for a moment as if she were jumping over a hurdle. His hand swept under her and through the air, and Evie landed back on the curving wall, sure-footed as a cat, now heading away from the path and toward the llama pasture.

She felt some relief, but as she glanced behind her she saw the wired-jaw man climb up onto the wall himself. The melted man was nowhere to be seen, and she realized he had probably opted to take the long route, through and around the park to the other side, where the llama pasture was open to the public. The thought distracted her, and she tripped. She flailed her arms about and she fell hard, hitting the side of her face on the wall, her hands on either side of it, but both her legs dangling precariously into the pit. She lay there for a moment, the pain in her cheek and knee throbbing, and then slowly pushed herself up to standing again.

As she rose to her feet and started to run again, feeling a bit wobbly, she was suddenly struck with a plan. It was dangerous and risky, but it might just work.

Evie slowed her pace a little. She needed the man to catch up with her, just a bit, just enough. She looked over her shoulder and saw him gaining ground. *Look scared, look worried,* she thought. Which wasn't too hard to do, really.

Seeing her supposed fear, the wired-jaw man sped up, and she slowed down just a tiny bit more. She judged the distance between them and then turned to look where she was going. It was now a guessing game, and it was very important that she guess right. She listened intently as the sound of his footsteps got louder and louder. They coincided nicely with her heartbeat getting louder and louder. *Just wait,* she told herself. *Just be patient.* . . . Louder and louder, faster and faster and . . .

Then, suddenly, Evie stopped. She crouched down, holding on tightly to each side of the wall. She kept her head tucked under and stared between her knees as the wired-jaw man tried to skid to a stop and barreled into her. He was heavy, and she tipped to one side but she held on as tightly as she could, keeping her center of gravity low. She heard a guttural strained grunt and then a kind of cry from somewhere deep in his throat. Evie turned and watched as the man fell into the bear pit, landing on a mushy pile of straw.

Evie stood up and looked into the pit. One down, but the melted man was still somewhere rushing to the llama pasture. And the wired-jaw man was already looking for a way out. He was trying to crawl up a series of boulders stacked on top of each other at the far end of the enclosure.

That definitely got her running again. Faster and faster, the field approaching in the distance. Her breath was short now, her muscles ached. But finally, *finally*, she made it to the field and jumped off the wall onto the wet grass. For a moment she enjoyed the relief, but she realized she still had a serious problem on her hands.

Not only was she being chased, but Sebastian, and maybe Catherine, too, was still in danger, locked up inside the Reptile Realm.

Locked up.

Evie remembered that the melted man had a key to the Reptile Realm. She saw him put it in his jacket pocket when they were spying. But how on earth was she going to get at it?

She felt trapped. Maybe she could go back? With the wired-jaw man climbing out of the bear pit with a gun still somewhere on his person, she didn't want to risk it. But she couldn't really go forward either, not with the melted man ready to greet her at the other end of the pasture. So she stood there for a moment.

She needed to escape. She needed to rescue.

And, *oh*.

Llamas.

➤ CHAPTER 17 ◄

In which there's a conversation and also llamas.

"I'm Sebastian," said Sebastian. It was a literal answer to Catherine's question, and he knew she wanted more, but he just didn't know where to start. All he really wanted to do was ask her about the key and Alistair and what had happened to the Filipendulous Five, but it didn't seem quite the moment for all that. Not yet.

"Okay. Sebastian. I suppose it's nice to meet you." Though Catherine didn't sound too sure.

"Nice to meet you too." It was only polite to reply in kind.

"Well, Sebastian, why are you here exactly?" asked Catherine.

"In the terrarium?" he asked.

"At the zoo," clarified Catherine. "Why are you here?" Catherine was looking at him with suspicion, and Sebastian was taken aback by that. He was, after all, only trying to help. Then again, he supposed, it wasn't like Catherine knew that.

"Oh, um, well, I'm here with Evie Drake," he said.

Catherine's eyes widened. "Drake?"

"Yes. She's Alistair Drake's granddaughter." Catherine and the snake both stared at him, not moving, not blinking. It was unnerving. So Sebastian continued to talk. "She got a letter from him saying he was in danger and that she needed to protect a key. How I come into the story is a bit complicated, but basically I'm helping her find you. So you can help her. Hopefully. Maybe."

More unblinking from the snake and the explorer.

"You were supposed to give a lecture last night," continued Sebastian, "and the old caretaker told us you were here and that you were summoned five days ago and we figured something was wrong. And we were right. And I have to say I'm really confused about what's going on right now. Are you in trouble or not?" He stopped talking and considered. Yes. That was it. That was all he wanted to say. If they could stare at him unblinking, he could stare back. No matter how watery his eyes got.

Fortunately Catherine only took a brief moment before replying. "Well, that's not good," she said slowly. "I don't know where Alistair is or what dangerous situation he might be in, but if he wants us to protect the key . . . and all week these men have been trying to scare me into revealing its location . . ." She stopped and looked at him sharply. "Maybe you're part of their plan."

"I'm not, I swear," he said, feeling insulted but also really excited that Catherine seemed to know where the key was.

"Well . . . ," she said in a tone that suggested she didn't altogether believe him, "I will never reveal what I know. They threw me in here with Penelope, thinking that would scare me, that she'd try to attack me, but she's just a darling and we've always got on. She became protective and I've been pretty much sitting here ever since. They can't kill me because they need information, and any time they come into the terrarium, Penelope lashes out at them. I just wish they'd come a little closer and let her bite them. Anyway, we've been at a bit of an impasse, shall we say." She reached up with her free arm and scratched the top of the python's head. The snake leaned back and looked at Catherine upside down, and she moved her hand to scratch under its chin. "Now you're telling me Alistair is in danger. . . ." Catherine looked off for a moment as if she was thinking. "Well . . . I suppose it's all beginning to make sense."

"We have to protect the key," said Sebastian.

"We have to rescue ourselves first," Catherine corrected him with a sad smile.

"Maybe Evie can do it," he said.

"Maybe."

Sebastian felt himself deflate, and he sat lower, picking up a piece of straw on the floor and playing with it mindlessly. "Except," he said, "except I saw those men go out to find her. With guns."

"Oh," said Catherine.

He almost felt like crying, which never really happened. But he was so worried for Evie. He looked at Catherine, who looked neither worried nor not worried; she just kind of *looked*. "She's in serious danger," he said.

The llama gave Evie a friendly shoulder bop with its head and she gave it a scratch behind its ears. She felt another bop in the small of her back and turned to see another llama making a similar request. Evie couldn't help but laugh, surrounded by so many tall, long-necked, fuzzy white creatures all wanting scratches and affection. They were generally a very friendly bunch, but Evie was hoping she was remembering her animal biology course from school correctly. She had read that llamas were quite territorial when it came to other males, though they liked females well enough. She had to hope that that went for human males as well.

She was standing near the low fence next to the path on the far side of the pasture, quite some distance away from the bear pit, but, as far as she could work out, near the melted man, who had yet to arrive. She

was a sitting duck. Or a standing human. Or an honorary llama. Or whatever. Just waiting. Hoping.

Her plan had to work or she was done for.

Fortunately she didn't have to wait long. The melted man turned the corner and ran toward the pasture. He was running fast but came to a sudden stop about fifteen feet away when he saw her in the middle of the herd of llamas.

"What is this?" he asked with a laugh.

"These are llamas," replied Evie.

He shook his head and hopped over the fence easily. Evie stayed put despite the fact that her heart was beating fast and her fight-or-flight response was definitely leaning more toward flight. Once again, as with the wired-jaw man on the wall, she was using herself as bait.

She decided she really didn't enjoy using herself as bait.

As the melted man approached, the llamas turned and looked at him. The largest one, the male, completely white except for one brown patch on the top of his head, wandered over in front of Evie and stood between her and the man. It stared off into the distance and chewed in the man's general direction.

"*Nice* llama," said the melted man with a bit of a

laugh, raising his hand to pet the animal. He placed his hand on the top of its head and, much to Evie's disappointment, the llama stayed put. "What a nice stupid beastie," he said, giving the top of its head a scratch.

The llama stared and chewed.

Then the llama spat.

He spat right in the melted man's face, and the melted man recoiled and stumbled backward. "You stupid animal!" he growled, wiping at his face. He pulled out his gun and aimed it at the llama and Evie gasped. Surely he wasn't about to kill the lovely creature. But she watched in relief as one of the llama's friends charged the man and hit him right in his ribs with its head. It so surprised the melted man that he was knocked off his feet, his gun flying out of his hand. More llamas surrounded him and started kicking at him and spitting, and Evie took the moment to give her plan a go. She dove into the herd and fell right on top of the man. He stared at her in shock for a moment and then she quickly reached into his left jacket pocket. It had to be somewhere on him. It had to be. For their part, the llamas were kind enough to keep their kicking to the melted man, though one struck her by mistake on her thigh, causing her to look up and wince from the pain. The culprit made a guttural trill by way of apology. There was no time to nurse her leg; she had to find the key. She shoved her hand into his right jacket pocket.

The key . . . the key . . .

Why was she always looking for a key . . . ?

The key!

She pulled herself up and the llamas closed in once more around the man. She turned and started running toward the low fence. She had to get back to the Reptile Realm as fast as she could before the melted man escaped. She felt so stupidly slow. Suddenly she sensed someone was keeping pace with her. Shoot. It was him. He'd made it out of the herd! She turned and was pleasantly surprised to see not a scary melted man, but the male llama jogging beside her. She stopped. The llama stopped. They looked at each other.

Or maybe . . .

CHAPTER 18

In which no one asks me to play the French horn. And also there's a daring escape.

"So how do we escape, then?" asked Catherine.

"We didn't really have one planned," admitted Sebastian, playing with his piece of straw and feeling more and more hopeless as the minutes ticked by.

Catherine sighed sadly. "I suppose that is typical of the young of any species. They don't tend to plan ahead."

"That's actually really untrue," said Sebastian, feeling defensive. "We've done really well . . . up until this point."

Catherine didn't say anything, just exchanged a look with Penelope that made Sebastian more angry. He stood up in a huff. "You know what? We didn't need to do any of this. I certainly shouldn't be here.

None of this is any of my business." He could feel the tears welling up, ready to burst forth, and it terrified him. "And now Evie's in serious danger, and when those men come back who knows what they'll do and—"

"Who's that?" asked Catherine, staring out of the terrarium.

Sebastian turned and saw Evie racing toward them. She stopped abruptly in front of the glass and placed her palms against it, staring at them wide-eyed. Sebastian flew over in pure relief and said loudly, so she could hear him through the glass, "You're okay!"

Evie grinned and held up a key.

"She can get us out of here!" said Catherine, sounding impressed.

"Yes!" said Sebastian, now feeling guilty he had been so worried that Evie was in danger and couldn't take care of herself when all this time she was being awesome. He pointed to the right. "The door's over there!" he said, and Evie nodded. She dashed out of sight and a moment later the door to the terrarium was flung open.

"You're okay!" she said.

"You're okay too!" he said.

"Okay, you two . . . young . . . people. Let's get out of here!" Sebastian turned and saw that Catherine was now standing, free from Penelope, who slithered up to Evie and gave her a once-over. For the first time Sebastian could see just how tall Catherine was—over six feet—and he was surprised how young she still looked. She had aged a little bit since the pictures, with small, almost imperceptible lines around her eyes and mouth, but otherwise she looked almost exactly the same as twenty years ago. Her hair was as brilliant red as ever, not a gray hair to be seen.

"Are you Catherine Lind?" asked Evie as Catherine walked over to the door. She said it with a slight almost-shyness, it sounded like.

"I am," replied Catherine, turning and looking at her. Her voice softened. "Evie Drake. You look just like your grandfather. But a female. And a kid. Like a baby goat." The two appraised each other for a moment, Evie staring at her with one of her classic unreadable expressions and Catherine looking her up and down with considerable interest as if she were a newly discovered species. Then Catherine said, "Okay, let's go." She turned to Penelope and gave her one final scratch. "Thank you, girl. You saved my life." Then the three of them ran out of the terrarium and through the main doors of the Reptile Realm.

The fresh air felt wonderful on Sebastian's face, but he had no time to enjoy it, fearing at any moment the men would reappear. All three of them continued apace, running past a llama standing on the side of the pathway, chewing. Sebastian gave it a quick look and then looked at Evie.

"He let me ride him back here. It's . . . a long story," she said, and Sebastian nodded. It must be.

They tore through the zoo as fast as they could. They turned onto the main thoroughfare and stopped short. Right by the gates stood the wired-jaw man, looking smugly proud of himself.

There's another exit. "This way!" said Sebastian, and he started down the small path that ran perpendicular to the gates. The man saw them and began chasing them.

"Where are you going?" called out Catherine.

"There's a side exit for school visits," Sebastian shouted back.

"Are you sure?" she yelled again.

"He's got a photographic memory!" Evie called out.

Why can't people just trust without questioning everything? wondered Sebastian. It was extremely frustrating. And sure enough, there it was, the side exit. And beyond it a street with some shops, with people even sitting on a patio for lunch. It was very strange seeing people just having a relaxing day after all they'd been through.

They burst out through the gates and turned down the street. Without really thinking too much about it, knowing that the wired-jaw man was still somewhere behind them, Sebastian quickly turned down a narrow alley and then, seeing a side entrance to a café, led Catherine and Evie inside. They burst into the packed café and came to a frantic stop. Then Sebastian collected himself and walked as casually as he could into the middle of the large crowd waiting for their drinks to be made, Catherine ducking down a little to disguise her height. Sebastian glanced out the front windows just in time to see the wired-jaw man fly by. Sebastian turned quickly and crouched right in front of a table of two teenagers. He stared at their black ankle boots and thick gray socks with red stripes for a moment.

And waited.

And waited.

Holding his breath in fear.

He looked ahead and saw Evie also on the ground.

"Hey, man, you okay?" asked one of the teens, bending down and looking at him.

"Oh yeah, sorry, I dropped . . . something. . . ."

"Okay. Cool."

More waiting.

More waiting.

How much more waiting?

And when would he be able to breathe again?

"Okay, kids, it's safe to stand up," said Catherine from above them. Her brown work boots came into view and Sebastian slowly stood up. "He's gone. For now."

Sebastian nodded and felt his heart calm to a more regular rhythm. He looked at Evie, who was pushing her hair back behind her ears.

"That's a relief," said Evie, and she walked over to Catherine. *That's an understatement,* thought Sebastian. "Now," she said, "I think we need to talk."

CHAPTER 19

In which great revelations are greatly revealed.

They found a small table at the back of the café, far away from any windows and well hidden by the crowd still standing around the counter, and ordered three hot chocolates. Evie honestly couldn't think of anything that had ever tasted better in her life. Maybe staring death in the face just made things tastier. She certainly didn't feel much like testing her theory any more than she just had, though.

"But you're both so young," Catherine was saying, still staring at them in confusion.

"Maybe, but we need to protect the key and save my grandfather," Evie said, wondering what being young had to do with anything. "We need you. It's as simple as that. My grandfather needs you," she added, making her voice more patient-sounding.

"Can't you just help us?" pressed Sebastian.

"Please." Evie opened her eyes as wide as they could go, trying to look as helpless and sweet as possible.

Catherine was quiet for a moment longer, and then,

when Evie felt like she was about to fall to her knees and pathetically beg in desperation, she said, "You look like a little puppy dog with that expression. I like puppies. I suppose when you think about it," she said almost to herself, "kids are a bit like puppies, really."

Evie wasn't sure where this train of thought was leading, but she hoped it was in their favor. Catherine smiled a small smile for the first time.

"I'm not great with humans," she confessed.

"Me neither," said Sebastian.

Catherine turned to him and, after a moment, nodded. "Well, I think first of all I need to understand more about what's going on here. Can I see this letter from Alistair?"

Evie felt a little nervous as she passed her grandfather's letter to Catherine. It was weird, but after all this effort trying to track down someone from the Filipendulous Five to help, she all of a sudden wondered if they were right to have done so. I mean, what did she really know about Catherine anyway? Could she be trusted? Still, what choice did they have?

"Wait. This can't be," said Catherine as she read the letter. She looked up at Evie in surprise. It was the first time she'd come across as truly thrown for a loop—not suspicious, not concerned, but honestly intrigued.

"What?" asked Sebastian.

"When did you get this?" Catherine quickly passed the letter back to Evie.

"Three days ago. But the Andersons got it last week," she replied.

"Yes, it's starting to make sense," Catherine said, thinking hard. "Alistair sent me a letter last week as well."

"What?" asked Sebastian, wide-eyed.

"Well, it really was nothing that pressing, just a regular letter. Once in a while I do get letters from the team, except Doris. She has completely vanished." Catherine seemed sad as she said it. "It mentioned nothing of being in trouble, which is why I found all this quite surprising at first, but now, reading this letter . . . I remember how mine was strangely phrased, not a usual 'this is what I'm up to these days' kind of thing. It was odd, I remember that. Then I thought maybe he was just getting a little long in the tooth, as it were. But now . . . now I think he wrote a hidden message in mine. I think . . . I could be wrong, but that bit about the four directions, it's too poetic really for him. . . ."

"'The four directions all point home,'" quoted Evie, reading the letter again herself. She looked up when she realized. "You say you got a letter. . . . Maybe you all got letters?"

"There is no way of knowing for certain right now, but . . ."

"The four directions, that's the four of you. All four of you got letters, and they all point to 'home.' They point to where Alistair is." Yes, that was it! It hadn't been a clue to find Benedict at all. It had been a clue to find her grandfather! Evie was starting to feel excited and hopeful again.

"I do believe so. I do believe he's asking all of us to save him," agreed Catherine. "And he gave us each some kind of clue that when combined with the others will tell us how to do so."

"Why would he do that? Why would he speak in riddles in the first place?" asked Sebastian, confused.

"I don't know." Catherine leaned back in her chair and furrowed her brow.

"Maybe," Evie said slowly. "Maybe so that no one letter could reveal where he was? Maybe . . ." She thought harder. All this time deep down she'd assumed that there had been a connection between the men and her grandfather. That the reason he was in danger had to do with them, that they maybe even had him prisoner or something. But she had actually never had any evidence of that at all. Maybe she'd been wrong. "Maybe I was wrong; these men don't have him at all. He's in danger somewhere else, trapped somewhere else, and the men are also looking for him. He's being careful so that if a letter fell into the wrong hands, they couldn't find him!" Her heartbeat was so loud in her throat she felt a need to speak over its thudding.

"Shh!" said Catherine quickly.

Evie nodded, glancing over her shoulder. Fortunately, no one in the café seemed to have noticed her outburst. It was so hard to contain it all, though; it was all making so much sense . . . except . . . No. No it wasn't. "But why would those men be looking for him at all?" she asked. "I mean, he doesn't have the key, and they clearly know that, so what does he have that they want?"

Catherine leaned forward in her seat and picked up her mug of hot chocolate. "His piece of the map," she said, then took a sip.

"His piece of what map?" asked Evie. This was new. There was a map, too?

Catherine took a moment, and then seemed to come to some kind of decision. "I think . . . yes, I think it's time to tell you the story," she said slowly.

"The story of what?" asked Evie.

"Of why the Filipendulous Five disbanded all those many years ago."

"Yes!" exclaimed Sebastian, practically jumping

out of his seat. This time a few people sitting at the table beside them glanced over at the noise. "I mean," he said, settling himself down, "yes, please. I'm very curious about that."

"Well," began Catherine after giving him a look, "our last expedition was meant to take us deep into the Mariana Trench. Do you know what that is?"

"I do!" said Sebastian, raising his hand high into the air. Evie shook her head. He was so delightfully odd sometimes.

Catherine looked confused. She pointed at Sebastian hesitantly. "Uh, yes . . . ," she said, "young boy?"

"*Sebastian,*" he reminded her. "I have the answer."

"Oh," Catherine said, puzzled. "Okay."

"The Mariana Trench is the deepest part of the Pacific Ocean. It is one of the last places on all the earth that hasn't been explored. No one knows what's down there."

"Yes, that's the Mariana Trench," said Catherine with a smile. "Well done, Sebastian the boy. Except you're wrong about one thing. It *has* been explored. By us." She looked away for a moment, almost seeming to forget the two of them were there.

"No, that's impossible. The trench is so deep in the ocean that no human has been able to reach its farthest depths." Sebastian sat with his mouth agape, and Evie thought it would have looked kind of funny if this weren't such a serious moment.

Catherine's expression seemed to grow darker, heavier. "It was to be the greatest exploration of all time. We built a special submarine for the venture, one that wouldn't be crushed under the weight of all the water on top of it, one that was able to dive to depths previously never humanly possible. We packed it up, we piloted it deep into the ocean, and we made our way into the dark unknown of the trench. The creatures that live down there, you cannot even imagine." Catherine's eyes got a little misty as she continued to look off somewhere into the distance. "It was a treacherous journey, and we almost didn't make it until we came upon something so completely bizarre it changed everything."

"What? What was it?" asked Sebastian, leaning forward.

"We suddenly found ourselves emerging out of the water. This was completely unexpected and seemed to defy all the laws of physics. But it happened. And before us was a waterfall, tall and shimmering in the light from our submarine. As we climbed out of the vessel, we were covered in its fine mist. I'd never felt more alive, more ready for whatever adventures might come my way. I felt ten years younger."

"Wait a minute," said Evie. She was starting to see where this story was going. Catherine nodded at her.

"Yes, whatever the water was, wherever we were, there was some kind of special property that made us feel younger and more alive."

"A fountain of youth," Evie breathed in awe.

"Well, no, not really. It wasn't a fountain, it was a waterfall. And we don't know if it made us actually younger or made us just feel that way. We took a sample and left. But we never got a chance to study it. On our journey back to the surface we encountered a beast unlike any I had ever seen before. Twice the size of the submarine, with sharp teeth and incredible strength. Also, despite its size, it was terribly agile and quick. It attacked our ship and we fought it. Fought it long and hard. The ship's structural integrity was compromised. We couldn't escape the beast, and none of our smaller weapons could pierce it. So finally we shot a missile at it."

"You have missiles?" said Sebastian, but Catherine ignored the question.

"The creature easily outmaneuvered the weapon, but the missile struck a rock wall behind it, showering large debris onto the beast and burying it. The result was our freedom, yes, but what we did not know until we surfaced was that the explosion into the rock had triggered an earthquake. The earthquake was so large that it had produced a tsunami that, by the time it reached land, washed out all the homes and businesses of a small island nation nearby."

"That's terrible!" said Evie, aghast.

"It was," said Catherine softly. She took a moment before she continued. "Everyone assumed it was caused naturally, but we knew the fault was ours. We did what we could. We gave them all the money we had earned over the years of exploring. We stayed for a year and a half, helped rebuild the island, and when it was done, when all our money had been spent, we had no desire to explore again. So much damage that did not need to have happened, just because we wanted to be the best, to discover all the secrets of the world. It was selfish."

"I'm so sorry," said Evie. It was hard to know what to do in a moment like this. Catherine looked incredibly sad, but it didn't seem as if she was the kind of person who liked hugs all that much. So Evie just sat there.

"We still had a vial of the water from that waterfall. No one could agree who should get it, and no one wanted to destroy it. We decided to split it up. We each took a fifth." Catherine reached into her shirt and pulled out a tiny vial on a chain. There was maybe a spoonful of water inside it at most. It didn't look particularly special, but Evie still marveled at it.

"Then we parted ways, to lead our own lives. We decommissioned the submarine and divvied up what remained of our tools. Only Alistair wanted to keep a proper record of our achievements. He created a puzzle box full of newspaper cuttings and pictures that only we could open." Evie glanced at Sebastian, who was looking a little smugly proud at that revelation. She didn't blame him. Catherine went on, "And he refused to destroy the map Benedict had made to the waterfall. It was his highest achievement, finding that waterfall, he said. I'd begged him to set fire to it, but Alistair wouldn't. I could see then how precious the map was to him, and I agreed we shouldn't burn it. But I said we should divide it up, like the water, cut it into six pieces, and then it would be safe."

"Six pieces?" asked Sebastian.

"Yes," replied Catherine, not seeming to understand the question.

"Why, if there are five of you?"

"The sixth piece was the 'key' to the map. The part of the map with explanations of what all the symbols meant . . ."

"The key!" gasped Evie, and she turned to look at Sebastian. He too was wide-eyed.

"Yes," replied Catherine, who looked a little taken aback by their reaction.

"The key! It's not a *key*. It's a 'key'! It's part of a map," said Evie. She was completely floored by the revelation.

"Correct. I thought you knew this."

"We didn't. We thought it was a key," said Sebastian.

"Okay . . ." Catherine just looked at him for a moment like he was crazy. Finally she turned back to Evie and said, "May I go on?"

"Oh yes, of course," said Evie, though she still couldn't get over it.

"We felt none of us should have the key in case anyone was tempted to try to use their piece of the map to find the waterfall. I couldn't imagine who would want to go back; it seemed a silly consideration after everything. Surely we were all done with it. But Doris was always the skeptic. And to be fair, she understands human nature far better than I do."

"What happened to the key?" asked Sebastian.

"They gave it to the Andersons," said Evie, suddenly understanding. All this time she'd thought the men had made a mistake coming to the house to find the key. That when Mr. Anderson had said "It's not here," he'd just been correcting them. But it wasn't the case at all. They'd once had the key. But they had gotten rid of it.

It was Catherine's turn to look surprised. "Yes. Yes, we did."

"But why the Andersons?" asked Evie. Finally she would understand the connection.

"The Andersons were our bankers," replied Catherine. "They handled all our finances. They were among the few who knew what really happened; they wired us our money so we could give it to the people of that island. They were highly trustworthy. Still are, apparently. Good people, always looked out for us."

Evie felt a little ashamed in that moment. That was why they had cared so much about her. Why they'd invited her to dinner regularly. All this time they hadn't been pitying her, as she'd assumed; they'd been looking out for her.

"So," said Sebastian carefully, "what you're saying is that Alistair has a part of this map. And we know he wants us to protect the key. The men are after the key. We know this because they demanded it of the Andersons. And if they want the key, they must want the map. So the men want to find the waterfall." Evie nodded along with each point.

"Yes," said Catherine. "That seems to be the case."

"And," added Evie, "my grandfather is in danger

and we have to rescue him. We don't know why or where, but there are clues that he sent to each of you guys. And if you each also have a piece of the map, and the men are after the map, then you are all in danger too." Yes, it all seemed just a little bit daunting, but Evie felt up to the task. She'd never felt more ready to prove herself worthy before. She would prove to her grandfather she was a Drake: brave, resourceful, and no stranger to adventure. She just would.

"That's a very accurate and terrifying summary of all we're facing. But as with any challenge, it's best to look at it piece by piece, and not as a whole. So. First things first, then," said Catherine. "Let's go to the Andersons' and get the key."

"They don't have it anymore," said Evie.

"They don't?"

"No, they said it wasn't there. Which I guess is good, because those men burned the house down. But where it is . . . well, that's the thing. That's what Sebastian and I have been trying to figure out. That's why we came to find you. Now that we know they had it once upon a time, though, that changes everything."

"They must have hidden it when they got this letter. They must have thought that was enough to protect it," said Catherine.

"Where would you hide a key if you were the Andersons?" asked Evie, of herself and to the others.

Everyone thought hard.

Come on, Evie, come on, you can do this. If all this time the Andersons had been protecting the key . . . What if what Mrs. Anderson had said in front of the tunnel was not about getting someone to help them find the key, but actually finding it itself? Evie looked up and stared at Catherine.

"I think I know where the key is." She turned to Sebastian, who stared back at her in wonder.

"Where?" he asked.

"It's so obvious. The Andersons must have thought it was too obvious and so no one would ever think of looking there."

"No," said Sebastian. Evie could tell he was putting it all together now. "No, you don't mean . . ."

"Yeah," she said, laughing a little in disbelief. "I'm pretty sure it's hidden at The Explorers Society."

CHAPTER 20

In which . . . Wait,
The Explorers Society?
Again?

"The Explorers Society?" asked Catherine, looking just as stunned as Sebastian felt.

"Yes," replied Evie.

"But where?" asked Sebastian. "The key wasn't in the box."

"What box?" asked Catherine.

"The puzzle box you were talking about, with all the Filipendulous Five stuff in it," replied Sebastian. "I found it. At the society headquarters. I work there, sort of. Or used to, anyway. That's how we found out about you."

Catherine gave a laugh in what appeared to be complete disbelief. She looked at Evie and then at Sebastian and then back again. "Who knew children could be so resourceful?" she said.

"I did," said Sebastian, really not enjoying her constant digs at their youth.

Catherine ignored his retort and turned to Evie. "So let's say the key is at The Explorers Society. That hardly tells us where specifically it is."

Evie sighed. "Yeah. It's a really big building with lots of rooms. . . ."

"And some rooms that haven't even been discovered yet," agreed Catherine.

Sebastian was slightly shaken by that but chose to ignore it for the time being. Instead he racked his brain; surely there was a clue hidden somewhere in there. He went through shelves of memories, looking at pictures of things he'd seen, anything related to the Filipendulous Five.

"I wonder if the president of the society or someone like that would know something," Evie said.

"Myrtle?" asked Sebastian, distracted by his own thoughts.

"The Ice Queen?" said Catherine with a grim smile. "Oh dear. I doubt she'd help us."

"Why not?" Sebastian was still not really focused on the conversation, tossing memories here and there, making quite a mess in his subconscious.

Catherine laughed.

"What is it?" asked Evie.

"Oh, don't get me wrong, I have a great deal of respect for her. But . . . well . . . when Alistair told her the truth about the earthquake, she was furious, and she expelled us from the society forever. She also removed any trace of our adventures, lest anyone get any bright ideas and be inspired by us. She wanted to destroy the puzzle box too, and the EM-7056, but she finally relented when Doris reminded her of the dangers of completely wiping out history."

Well, that explained why she had reacted so badly when Sebastian had questioned her. Wait a minute. . . . Sebastian focused on that moment, the one in the tree house when she'd looked like she was about to explode: *The door is locked and the key hidden.*

"I think Myrtle has the key," said Sebastian, surprised. He stared at Catherine and Evie, who looked very much the way he felt.

"Are you sure?" asked Evie.

"Pretty sure. Not certain. It was something she said before she kicked me out. But it makes so much sense. You say she erased your existence from the society. The Andersons likely would have asked the president for help. She would have wanted to keep it secret. The only thing is . . ."

"What?" asked Evie, sitting at the edge of her seat.

"She might have destroyed it."

Evie's face fell as Catherine nodded. "She might have," said Catherine. "But maybe not. After what Doris said, I think she's more respectful of artifacts."

"Plus," added Evie, "maybe the Andersons explained how vital it was that she *not* destroy it."

"What do we do, then?" asked Sebastian. "We clearly can't just ask Myrtle where it is."

Catherine shook her head. "No, considering I've been banished, I don't think she'd like seeing me again," she said.

"And considering she kicked me out just because of who my grandfather is . . . ," added Evie.

"And when I asked Myrtle about the team, she kicked me out too . . . ," said Sebastian.

"Okay, so somehow we have to find the key without Myrtle's help," said Evie.

Catherine looked at her. "Pretty much."

Evie sighed. "Well, this shouldn't be challenging at all."

"Really? Because it seems very challenging to me," replied Sebastian.

"Indeed," agreed Catherine. "In fact, I'd say it's a monumental task."

Evie sighed hard. "Okay, so I wasn't being serious there. . . . Anyway, the point is, let's go and find this key!"

They made their way out of the café and caught the local bus. It took half an hour to get to the stop near The Explorers Society, and on the journey they all decided the best course of action was to sneak in and head right for Myrtle's private office. She was almost never there, and Sebastian thought it was worth the risk. If she caught them . . . well . . . they'd have to figure something out in the moment, they supposed. Sebastian at least still had his keys to the building, so they hoped to be able to slip inside without being noticed.

"I haven't been here in years," said Catherine, staring at the sign for the society. She reached up and touched it delicately with her fingers and shook her head a little. "I used to love it here."

"It *is* pretty amazing," agreed Sebastian.

"Well," Catherine said, pulling her hand back suddenly, almost as if she'd gotten a shock, "no more of this. Let's go."

Sebastian unlocked the door and they all sneaked inside. They closed it and turned to see Hubert standing there looking at them. But he nodded happily, as if they were all supposed to be there, and wandered off.

"He's the one who let me in the first time," whispered Evie.

"Oh! That makes sense, then. He's definitely pretty clueless. I bet he recognizes Catherine and assumes she's still a member," said Sebastian.

"Very probably," said Catherine.

Sebastian pushed a few buttons on the wall and the elevator shot up to the sixth floor.

"It's just down here," whispered Sebastian as they arrived at Myrtle's office. He stood for a moment, worried that the door might be locked. But the doorknob turned and he was relieved that generally the people in the society were pretty trusting.

The door opened into a room painted a pale blue. The walls were covered in pictures from Myrtle's many expeditions to the Arctic—or they seemed to be pictures of her. They were, at the very least, pictures of a person in a bright orange snowsuit and goggles waving at the camera. The floor was covered from wall to wall in a plush blue carpet, and sitting in the middle was a white desk shaped like an iceberg. It was huge and took up most of the room, and it had numerous small drawers. Sebastian had never been in Myrtle's office before, and to say he was impressed would have been an understatement.

"Let's not waste any time," said Catherine, and each of them immediately chose a side of the iceberg and started riffling through the drawers. Sebastian

was a little disappointed that he had to look through them so quickly. He really wanted to examine their contents, which were extremely well organized and labeled. Myrtle evidently was fond of collecting rocks, and drawer after drawer revealed flat dull gray stones, each with a printed label naming it, like SLATE, GRANITE, FRANK, and JOSHUA.

"Anything?" asked Evie.

"Just a bunch of rocks," said Sebastian as he continued to open the drawers.

"I've found snowflakes," said Evie. "Well, I've found empty drawers with labels that *say* SNOWFLAKE on them," she corrected herself.

"Nothing here either," said Catherine. They all stood and stared at the desk.

There had to be something more, thought Sebastian. Then again, she could have hidden the key anywhere in the building, he supposed.

"Where else would she have put it?" asked Evie.

"I was just wondering the same thing," replied Catherine.

"What's this?" asked Sebastian, and he pulled a small, well-camouflaged white lever disguised as an artistic iceberg-like outcropping in the desk.

There was a sound from below as some kind of

machinery turned on. All three of them took a step backward and looked at each other in surprise. "What did you do?" asked Catherine.

"I pulled a lever," replied Sebastian, a little louder, as the sound was growing along with his unease.

"Without knowing what it did?" asked Catherine.

Now that she put it that way . . . But at the time it had just been instinct. Gut instinct. Something he hadn't realized until this moment he had. He glanced at Evie, who was still going through one of the drawers. "I guess so, yes."

Well, now he was feeling downright foolish, but . . . but . . . He lost his train of thought as he realized that the desk before him had suddenly started to grow taller and taller and taller. More iceberg appeared from within the floor and revealed itself to them. More drawers within the iceberg too. The three of them stood and watched it grow until the top of the desk was touching the ceiling. Then the mechanical noise stopped, as did the rising desk.

"I guess that was just the tip," said Evie with a shrug.

The three of them wasted no time and frantically began searching all the newly produced drawers, but all Sebastian found on his side were tea things. Drawers full of exotic tea. Drawers full of teacups. Drawers full of teapots. It was quite the collection.

"Anybody?" he called out.

"Cat toys," replied Catherine.

"Biscuits," said Evie.

"This is getting ridiculous," said Sebastian as he opened another drawer, this one full of spoons.

"I wonder," said Evie, sitting on the plush carpet to think, "if this even makes sense. If I had something I didn't want anyone else to get hold of, I'd probably keep it with me. Like your vial." She looked up at Catherine.

"Good point. Maybe she has it on her," replied Catherine.

"Any thoughts, Sebastian?" asked Evie.

Oh, he had thoughts, many thoughts, but none of them was useful. Most of them had something to do with "I shouldn't be here." There was one that went, "Wait, why am I still helping Evie when we've found Catherine?" Then there was another one that went, "Looking at all this tea is actually making me thirsty."

"Tea," he said. And he looked at Evie. "She's always serving tea."

"It definitely looks as if she likes to do that, doesn't it?" replied Evie.

"But I've never seen her actually pour the tea. It's always just there. Ready to drink. I think . . . I think I know where the key is." Sebastian turned and flew out of the office toward the elevator. He could hear Evie and Catherine following him, and sure enough, they stepped onto the elevator platform next to him.

"Where are we going?" asked Evie.

"To the tree house."

They ran out of the elevator and up the stairs, bursting through the rooftop door and into the warm light of the setting sun. In the distance Sebastian could see Myrtle sitting in the tree with David Copperfield on her lap. She hadn't noticed them yet.

"What do we do?" asked Evie.

"Let me talk to her," replied Catherine.

Before Sebastian could reply—because he certainly wondered if this was the best idea—Catherine was walking toward the tree. Sebastian and Evie followed slowly, and when they were making their way across the skylight roof, Catherine called, "Hi, Myrtle."

Myrtle turned and looked. Her eyes widened in horror. She stood quickly, David Copperfield falling onto the table.

"I'm not here to make trouble," said Catherine, holding her hands up. "I just want to talk."

"No, you want the key back. I knew this day would come," said Myrtle. "I knew you lot couldn't resist giving it another shot, no matter what the cost."

"It's not like that, Myrtle," said Catherine. Myrtle walked to the edge of the platform and stared down at Catherine, turning her body away from Sebastian and Evie.

"Other side," whispered Evie into Sebastian's ear.

Sebastian turned to look at her. She gave him a subtle nod and glance, and he turned to see where she was looking. The rope ladder on the other side of the platform peeked through the branches of the tree. Yes. Other side!

As quickly and quietly as he could, Sebastian ducked under the platform and maneuvered his way around the thick tree trunk. He grabbed the rope ladder behind it and slowly started to climb. When his head popped up above the platform, he ducked instinctively and then slowly raised it again.

"No? What other reason would you have to come here, then, after you and your offensive team were officially expelled from the society?" Myrtle was saying.

"It isn't about the team. It's about Alistair," said Catherine.

"And if Alistair isn't the team, I don't know who is." Myrtle glowered at her.

Sebastian climbed as stealthily as he could onto the platform. David Copperfield, now sitting on the table, turned and stared at him. Sebastian put a finger to his lips and then realized that the cat had no idea what that meant. It was, after all, a cat. He lowered his hand. He crept toward the table, the familiar flowery teapot sitting in the middle. He reached out, and David Copperfield watched as Sebastian grabbed the teapot and lifted it into the air. He pulled the pot toward him and opened it. It was empty. Well, that wasn't entirely true. It was empty of tea. What it was full of was key.

Sebastian could hardly believe it. His hands were shaking so much that the teapot also quivered. But he didn't have time to marvel at the discovery. He quickly pulled out the folded piece of paper, and just as he did, David Copperfield launched himself at him with a hiss. Sebastian dropped the teapot and it smashed into tiny pieces as he attempted to dislodge the cat, whose claws were firmly latched on to his shirt, and part of his flesh as well. Sebastian yelped in pain.

Of course all this noise made Myrtle turn around to witness the chaos.

"You!" She glared at him ferociously. "How dare you!"

Sebastian really couldn't say much of anything as he fought the cat on the platform, trying in vain to pluck the hissing beast off his chest. His heel caught the edge of the platform and he was suddenly falling backward. Apparently sensing that his own life was in danger, David Copperfield released Sebastian, flew over his head, and landed down a ways on the skylight roof, spinning to a frantic stop on his feet in the predictable cat way. Sebastian, on the other hand, landed flat on his back.

He took a moment to register the pain from the fall and the headache that now thudded in his brain, and he unfolded the paper. He stared at it. There was a large square drawn on the paper, and within it a series of symbols. Next to each symbol was an equals sign and an explanation of what that symbol meant. There were so many of them, and the piece of paper itself was quite large. He wondered how huge the entire map put together must be. He stared and stared and suddenly remembered the dire situation he was in when a hand grabbed for the paper as if to wrench it from his grasp.

He held to it fast: No! He wasn't losing it after just having found it!

"That's mine!" said Myrtle.

"No it's not," said Sebastian, struggling to keep hold of the paper while at the same time not ripping it.

"Well, it isn't yours!" she answered, and that, at least, was true.

"It doesn't belong to any of you. It belongs to us, the Filipendulous Five!" said Catherine, she and Evie joining them on their side of the tree.

"My grandfather!" said Evie.

And then, oddly, a fifth voice suddenly joined the conversation:

"Yet all this is utterly irrelevant, as you are going to give it to me right now."

➤ CHAPTER 21 ◄

In which somehow those men have found them, though I have no idea how and I'm just as flabbergasted as you are.

It was enough of a shock that all four of them—oh heck, all five of them, if you include David Copperfield, and I always try to—turned slowly toward the entrance to the rooftop. The two men were standing at the edge of the cobblestone path just before the glass skylight. Both aimed distinctly old-fashioned-looking guns at them, though of course only the melted man spoke.

Myrtle released the paper at the sight of the men and Sebastian scrambled to his feet, stuffing the key in his pocket.

"Who are you and what do you want?" demanded Myrtle. She stood defiantly, with her hands on her hips, David Copperfield at her side.

The melted man laughed. "My name is Mr. K and this is my colleague Mr. I, and we want that key to the map," he said.

"You can't have it," replied Myrtle.

There was an explosion as Mr. K fired the gun and the tree beside Myrtle splintered, raining little wooden bits onto their heads.

Sebastian instinctively ducked and noticed Evie doing the same beside him. Myrtle didn't flinch.

"I have a gun," Mr. K pointed out.

"Fascinating," replied Myrtle. Sebastian was amazed at how little she seemed bothered by the information. "I have a button." She slammed the palm of her hand into a knot of the tree that truly seemed natural and very knotlike. "Hold on to your hats!" she called out, and since no one was wearing a hat, Sebastian took it to be a turn of phrase that meant . . .

Oh. The skylight was dropping out from beneath him.

That was what she meant. They were all about to fall to their deaths.

Great.

As Evie felt the floor fall out from beneath her feet, she couldn't help but watch Mr. I and Mr. K staring at her. She really ought to have been looking down to see where on earth she would land, but the men so frightened her that she had a morbid curiosity about them. Gravity waits for no one, so her view was brief, but what she did see before she began to plummet were two men rushing toward them looking completely shocked. Mr. K fired his gun once more, but the bullet flew easily over their heads as Evie finally looked down.

The massive trunk of the tree curled this way and that below them and she thought she might possibly grab a passing branch, but as she reached out, another one appeared out of nowhere and smacked her right in the jaw, sending a sharp pain through her body. It forced her to flail out blindly, hoping she'd catch something. Suddenly her right hand connected with a thin branch and she grabbed on. It stopped her fall, though she slid along the branch, feeling a horrible burning sensation as the bark ripped at her skin. Finally she slowed to a stop and reached up with her other hand to get a better grip. This strategy took the weight off the one arm and she hung there, feeling a little useless, trying to get her bearings.

Her muscles screamed as she strained to keep her grip.

She glanced up and saw the men staring down through the hole. That was pretty terrifying. Then they were jumping through the hole. That was prettier terrifying.

Shoot, thought Evie, and just as she did, one of the men fired a gun. *That wasn't an order, that was an expression of frustration!* she thought in their general direction, but of course that was silly. No one in the vicinity was a mind reader, after all. She hoped.

Evie knew she had to get out of there. She hooked her legs over the branch. Then, upside down and sloth-like, but with more speed, she pulled herself along the branch toward the fifth-story library balcony. Another gunshot—this one hit the trunk of the tree above her. Evie glanced down—the balcony was right there, and Catherine was dangling dangerously from it, struggling to pull herself up. Evie inched closer and grabbed the balcony railing, heaved herself over it to safety, and rushed to help Catherine. As she did, another shot rang out, but it didn't sound so near her now. She thought then that maybe the men weren't actually shooting at her.

And that was when she realized they were shooting at Sebastian.

After all, he had the key.

≻ CHAPTER 22 ≺

In which there is much action and I still don't get to play my French horn.

Sebastian stared down at the floor of the library, which seemed to be swaying back and forth below him. Of course, Sebastian knew such a blatant defiance of physics could never occur, and took stock of what had happened. It took him less than that moment to realize that he was the one swaying, not the floor, and he turned to look above him. It was difficult to see exactly what was going on, but he was able to determine that his shirt had caught on something and he was dangling precariously over quite a drop. Whatever he was hooked onto had pretty much saved his life.

Sebastian looked left and saw a long tan-colored shape. Then he turned to his right and saw the same thing. His mind instantly flipped through images of the library from a few days earlier. And then he saw it. There it was.

The plane. He was hooked onto the scale model of the Wright brothers' plane, which was hanging angled slightly downward as if in midflight. If he could reach up, he could pull himself onto the wings and have a relatively sturdy platform to walk on.

The loud explosion of a gunshot sent slivers of tree raining down on him, and Sebastian realized this was a time for action, not contemplation. He turned to look behind him and saw one of the thin connecting supports between the top and bottom parts of the wing just a foot away from him. Like the bars of a prison cell, these supports ran the length of the wing, and Sebastian knew he could use them to heave himself up. He stretched his left hand behind him and felt around until he finally grasped the support. Then he took a deep breath as he reached up to the back of his shirt. He pulled down hard on the shirt, ripping it free, and he swung forward, holding on tightly with his left hand. As he swung back up he grabbed another support and thanked his lucky stars he was near enough the middle of the plane that he was able to do so. For one thing, it meant the plane was balanced with his weight, and for another, the supports were closer together at this point of the structure. Carefully, but as quickly as he could, he brought himself up onto the wing and crawled over to the pilot's area. He was breathing heavily and realized that maybe gym class hadn't been as much of a waste of time as he'd once thought. Certainly he now understood the value of chin-ups.

Sebastian looked to the left, then to the right. He couldn't see Evie, Catherine, or Myrtle anywhere. He wasn't sure if that was a good thing or a bad thing. He couldn't see above him since the top wing blocked his view, so he had no idea where the scary men were, though he could hear strange sounds of frantic chaos around him, which were utterly meaningless. He stuck his hand in his pocket. The key was still there. He pulled it out and stared at it one more time. Then he hastily put it away, realizing that the key was provoking butterflies in his stomach and a general sensation of excitement.

Another loud explosion and the plane swayed dangerously. Sebastian lay down on his stomach to steady himself. The plane turned ninety degrees to the right, causing his insides to slosh about dangerously, and for the first time he caught a glimpse of Catherine and Evie. They were below him, standing on the balcony in front of the "Linguistics and the Art of Alphabetizing" section. "Hey!" he called out to them. "I'm up here!"

Catherine looked around in confusion, but Evie turned and looked right at him.

"We need to get out of here!" she called back.

"I know!" replied Sebastian.

"Get down as fast as you can!"

"I'm not sure how exactly—" he started to say, as another shot rang out and Evie cried: "Duck!"

Sebastian ducked for cover, instinctively holding his hands over his head. The plane suddenly lurched, and the lurch was followed by a terrifying crack.

He heard Evie yell, "Sebastian!" just as he realized what was happening. The plane had broken free of its chain and was now flying solo. Sebastian held on for dear life as the plane started to fall toward the floor far below. This was it; this was his doom. And then he remembered, *I'm in a plane.*

Quickly he grabbed the lever in front of him and pulled back. The plane leveled out, and Sebastian sighed with relief only to realize he might not be falling down as steeply, but he was still flying forward and at quite a speed, and, oh, look, a wall.

Once more Sebastian ducked, right as the plane crashed into the fourth level of the library. Books exploded toward him and piled onto the plane and over his curled-up body. He stayed still, wrapped up in his own little world of darkness, until things got quiet; then he slowly pushed himself upright, a waterfall of books pouring off his head and back, and looked around. The nose of the plane was facing upward on an angle leaning on the balcony of the fourth level, and its tail stuck out, aiming toward the floor. As carefully as he could, and holding his breath, he pulled himself out of the books, sending more of them backward, and with a giant lurch, the nose of the plane tipped upward even more. Slowly, slowly . . . he stepped onto the wing and the plane slid a couple of inches backward, sending him stumbling forward. He grabbed on to a support and took stock of his new precarious situation. The plane leaned forward a bit and Sebastian took advantage of the moment to jump off the wing and onto the balcony, holding tight to a bookshelf for support. He turned and watched as the plane, now without his body weight, slowly started to slip backward, inch by inch picking up steam, until it finally slid off the balcony and fell to the floor with a thundering crash. Sebastian wanted to peek over the edge to see what had happened, but as he looked across the way to the other side of the library, he saw Mr. I aiming a gun right at him. Instinctively Sebastian held up the first book he could find and covered his head right as the shot was fired. The bullet didn't pierce the book, but its momentum did force the book right into Sebastian's face, and he heard a sickening cracking sound as the book met the bridge of his nose.

Sebastian was stunned by the pain and could taste salty blood in his mouth but didn't waste a moment feeling sorry for himself. He ran along the balcony to the nearest open door and flew inside. At this point he reached up and tenderly felt his nose. It hurt. A lot. And when he pulled his hand away, it was covered with blood. He looked at the book he was holding—*A Guide to Metalworking: How to make everything from streetlamps to book covers.* Ah, he noticed for the first time, the cover of this particular book was made of steel. How awfully convenient.

Sebastian turned around to find an exit and realized to his horror that he was in the human kinesiology room. The one full of bodies without their skin, posed doing various activities. It wasn't the creepy nature of the room that horrified him, but more the knowledge that there was only one way into and out of that room.

A dead end with dead people.

How horribly perfect.

➤ CHAPTER 23 ◄

In which meanwhile.

"We need to get to him!" Evie said to Catherine as she watched Sebastian escape through a doorway. Just when she had felt a flash of relief, everything had gone terribly wrong. As she was helping Catherine climb over the railing, Evie looked up to see Sebastian crash into the side of the library in what she was pretty sure was the Wright brothers' plane. Her heart had almost burst at the sight of Mr. I shooting Sebastian, but thank goodness for that marvelous book that seemed to be able to stop bullets for some reason. Still, he was in so much danger, and it was all her fault.

"I agree," replied Catherine, "but first we need to retrieve the EM-7056."

"Right. The EM-7056." Evie recalled Catherine

briefly mentioning it at the café earlier, but at the time they'd been focused on the key. "What exactly *is* the EM-7056?"

"It's the main source of power for the submarine. There is only one reason those fools want the key to the map: to get to the waterfall. And there is only one way to get to the waterfall: our submarine." Catherine started to jog around the balcony to the nearest exit, and for Evie that meant sprinting to keep up with the woman's long strides. "What do you know about underwater exploration?" asked Catherine, opening the door and letting Evie pass through into a darkened hallway.

"Not a lot. All we've really learned about underwater in school so far is fish," replied Evie, panting as she ran. They arrived at the elevator and jumped aboard. Catherine pressed a button and they rode in silence until they hopped off three floors up, and once again Catherine began to jog. Evie wondered if Catherine was disappointed that she didn't know anything about underwater exploration and that was why she stopped talking, but as they burst into a long, narrow room with wooden lockers running the length of one wall, Evie decided it didn't really matter.

"Where are we?" she asked.

"Underwater exploration is extremely difficult because the deeper you go, the more pressure all that water puts on a submarine," Catherine explained, making her way along the row of lockers. She arrived at one that had a large piece of paper with bright red writing taped to it. It read: "Do not open. The contents of this locker are extremely dangerous and mildly offensive. Anyone found opening this locker will be immediately expelled from the society. No joke."

Catherine tore the paper off the locker and fiddled with its combination lock. Evie took a deep breath and held it as Catherine pulled the latch and flipped open the locker. But there was nothing remotely scary inside. Just a rich-green leather jacket and a bullwhip.

Catherine took out the jacket and felt around inside it. Her hand slipped into an inner pocket and she sighed with relief. Turning to Evie, she said with a smile, "It's still here."

"What is?"

Catherine stared at her for a moment and then said slowly, like it was the most obvious thing in the world: "My part of the map." And she withdrew a piece of parchment.

Evie stared at it in wonder. She'd forgotten that each of the Filipendulous Five had a piece of the map. She had been so preoccupied with the key. "Can I look at it?" she asked.

Catherine shook her head and put the map back

into the pocket. "Not now. Later. When there's time."
She slipped on the jacket and reached into the locker,
pulling out the whip. Then she slammed the locker shut
and turned to Evie, looking rather impressive now.

"What's with that?" asked Evie, pointing.

Catherine glanced at the whip. "It's a whip," she
replied.

"Oh," said Evie. That wasn't what she'd meant by
asking the question. But it was her fault; she should
have been more specific.

"What were we talking about?" Catherine asked.

Evie, completely distracted at this point, couldn't
remember. "I don't remember."

"Ah, right, underwater exploration," replied Catherine. She turned and made her way back out of the
locker room, with Evie close behind. "Well, the deeper
you go, the more water gets piled up on top of whatever the object is, and even though water moves all
about, it's actually really dense." They stopped for a
moment as Catherine looked up and down the hallway, and then they quickly turned right.

"So you have a lot to deal with when trying to
make a journey like that. And you have to find a
way to make your submarine not fall apart under all
that pressure. No one had been able to build such a
ship. Until us," Catherine continued. "Doris came up

with this marvelous invention that created an electro-magnetic shield that allowed the ship to dive to such depths. And the bit that makes it run is hidden here at the society headquarters."

"It is?" said Evie, finally understanding where the conversation was going.

Catherine nodded. "Headquarters is, after all, the safest place to hide things."

"What else did you hide here?"

"Oh, that's it: our puzzle box, the key, my bit of the map, and the EM-7056. It might be safest to hide things here, but only a fool keeps everything in the same place," replied Catherine.

"Okay," said Evie. She supposed that made sense. They burst into a large, comfortable-looking room filled with different kinds of leather chairs. She re-membered it from the other day when she had first arrived here, and she realized all of a sudden just how very tired she was, how long a day it had already been, how long the one was before that, and how much all she wanted to do was sit in one of the comfy chairs before her. Running away from bad guys really does take it out of you.

But Catherine wasn't stopping anytime soon, so Evie rallied herself. Time for a second wind.

She caught up with Catherine as she was crossing

the length of the large room. "So where is the EM-7056 hiding?" Evie asked as they approached a glass case that sat between two tall windows. "Oh, is there a secret back to this case, like the filing cabinet Sebastian found the box in?" she asked as Catherine opened the doors. Catherine grabbed a gold metal orb that looked about the size of a grapefruit off its pedestal. Then she turned to Evie.

"Hold on to this. Don't lose it," she directed. Evie nodded and took the orb. It was smooth and cold to the touch. Very cold.

"What is this?" she asked, following Catherine back across the room.

"What do you mean? I just told you," replied Catherine.

"I just . . ." Evie looked at the orb. It didn't look all that impressive. "Wait. This isn't the EM-7056, is it?"

"Of course it is," replied Catherine, once more holding the door open for her.

"But it wasn't hidden at all. It was just there, in plain sight. Just sitting there." Evie was so terribly confused.

"The best place to hide something is in plain sight," said Catherine, dashing out into the hallway. Evie followed her. They both stopped. Evie stared at Catherine, who stared ahead silently, and it seemed they were both unsure what to do next.

"Let's get to Sebastian," suggested Evie, and Catherine nodded.

That was exactly the moment when the wall beside Catherine exploded. Evie jumped back, her heart pounding. "Get down!" yelled Catherine, and Evie flattened herself on the floor like a pro, shielding the orb underneath her body. She was getting really good at this duck-and-cover business.

She turned to look at Catherine for further instructions and watched her unfurl the bullwhip and swing it high over her head. There was a yell and then a thud, and Catherine leapt over Evie's body. Evie turned and saw Mr. K on the ground, scrambling for his weapon. But Catherine got there first. She grabbed the gun and pushed something along its grip, and its magazine full of bullets slipped out onto the floor. She then shoved the gun into her waistband at the back of her trousers just as Mr. K crawled to his feet and pulled out a knife.

By this point Evie was on her feet as well, frozen in place as Catherine came running toward her. Not wanting to let her down, Evie found her footing and was quick to fall in with her. They sped down the hallway as Catherine wound up her whip. Evie wasn't sure where they were going or what they were looking for. Catherine skidded to a stop in front of a door. Evie gave it a try. Locked. She gulped and looked up at Catherine.

"Next one," said Catherine. Evie nodded and they ran to the next one. Also locked. Evie was getting sincerely anxious. Mr. K was gaining ground, and Evie could see Catherine was preparing to use the whip again. She ran to the next door, grabbed the knob, and it opened. Relief!

"Catherine!" she called out, proud of her discovery, and the woman turned and gave her a sharp nod. Then she ran toward her.

Evie dove into the room and Catherine slammed the door behind them, locking it as she did. They both turned and stared at the door for a moment. They saw the doorknob rattle. The rattling stopped. Suddenly there was a loud thud on the other side, and another . . . and then there was silence.

Silence can be rather ominous and intimidating at the best of times. In this situation it was downright threatening. But even more threatening? A scary man all in black with half of his face melted off, including his ear, suddenly reciting a popular nursery rhyme on the other side of the door in a sickeningly sweet voice: "Little pig, little pig, let me come in!"

"Well, that doesn't top the creepy meter or anything," said Evie.

"Do you have such a tool of measurement on you?" replied Catherine, looking down at her.

"Boy, you and Sebastian really don't understand sarcasm, do you?" sighed Evie.

Catherine shrugged. "I guess not. I never really thought about it before."

Before Evie could answer there was another loud thud against the door. "Help me find something we can use as a barricade," Catherine instructed.

Evie nodded. They turned around, only then realizing how intensely pink the room was, lit as it was at one end by a large neon sign shaped like an ampersand.

And also only then realizing they were very much not alone.

"Little pig, little pig, let me come in!" said Mr. K yet again from behind the door.

"Snort" was the reply from the pig in the teeny hat.

➤CHAPTER 24◄

In which also meanwhile.

As quickly as he could, Sebastian ran and hid himself behind the body of Jonathan Llyr, the famous Shakespearean actor sitting in the classic Hamlet pose, just as Mr. I entered the human kinesiology room. The actor's body was seated and gave the most area behind which Sebastian could hide himself. He was just down to the left of the door and could see a little of the shadow of Mr. I. The man was standing in the doorway.

Sebastian watched as Mr. I's feet began to walk in his direction. This wasn't good, this wasn't good at all. Sebastian looked around. He couldn't hide himself forever. Mr. I knew he was in there. He had nowhere to go but deeper into the room, and that didn't make any sense. What he had to do was make a run for it. But Mr. I was standing between him and the exit. Sebastian dared to stand just a bit to see if he could see more of Mr. I, until he found himself face to face with Jonathan Llyr's head. The head the actor was holding in his hand in the Hamlet-holding-Yorick's-skull pose. Mr. I's shadow came closer. Sebastian stared at the head. The head stared back.

Sebastian put down his book.

Then he took a deep breath and grabbed the head and jumped in front of Mr. I.

"Catch!" Sebastian yelled, and threw the head at Mr. I, who instinctively dropped his gun and caught the head in his hands, staring at it, horrified. In that moment of confusion, Sebastian made a run for it. He darted through the door and back into the bright library. Directly opposite, on the far side of the room across the chasm below him, was a door that led to the hallway. All he had to do was run around the balcony to it. He turned left and started running until he reached the end of that side of the library and took a right. Just as he stepped forward, the railing shattered beside him. Mr. I had gotten his gun back, judging from the shards of railing all over Sebastian's front, and he'd clearly resumed the chase. Sebastian turned to look. Mr. I had evidently taken a right out of the room with the bodies and was now on the balcony that ran parallel to Sebastian across the other side of the library. Sebastian started running again, staying as low as he could, trying to use the railing of the balcony as some small protection. Oh, this was so not fun at all. So. Not. Fun.

He got to the door to the hallway and slid through it just as he saw Mr. I coming at the door from the other side. Sebastian ran into the darkened corridor and blinked hard, trying to adjust his eyes to the darkness. The elevator was at the other end of the building and the stairs were to his right, but far off. Which should he risk? His body made the decision for him, which was something like *Neither,* and he found himself opening a door a little down the hall and staring at a hole before him.

The slide. *Wow, body, good job,* congratulated Sebastian's brain. *No time for that, brain,* replied his body, and he launched himself down the slide. It was a moment of conflicting feelings as Sebastian enjoyed the rush of sliding and twisting, and was deeply thankful he'd found a way to safety, but then heard the distinct thump of someone climbing onto the slide behind him. Suddenly relief returned to fear, and Sebastian tried to make himself as aerodynamic as possible. *Must go faster,* he told his body, pulling his arms in and tucking his chin tight to his chest. He shot out of the mouth of the slide and into the foam pit, landing awkwardly, head down and feet in the air. Frantically, he clambered around, trying to pull himself up but sinking deeper into the pit instead as the large foam pieces compressed under his weight. This was utterly ridiculous. Finally he righted himself just as Mr. I came flying out and landed, just like Sebastian, head down, feet sticking up out of a pit of foam pieces. Sebastian struggled against the yellow blocks—he tried to drag his arms through them as if he were swimming; he pulled his knees up to kneel on top of one and sank deeper into the abyss, only to reach out and slip forward. Finally he just decided enough was enough and he grabbed the foam pieces in front of him, picked them up, and put them behind him. He grabbed the next ones and did the same. Yup, this was completely ridiculous.

Sebastian glanced over at Mr. I, whose arms had now appeared above the foam, flailing about a bit. Good. He was having problems too, and he was much larger than Sebastian, so surely his body weight would cause him even more trouble. The man's head finally emerged. He looked wildly about and saw Sebastian, then paused as if feeling around for something. He grunted loudly and Sebastian realized the man had dropped his gun. Mr. I began thrashing through the foam, hunting for his weapon, and Sebastian renewed his efforts at getting the heck out of there. He kept an eye on the man and watched as he seemed to resign himself to having lost his weapon and then turned and directed all his attention to Sebastian.

Must go faster.

Thus began one of the strangest and slowest chases in recent history.[12] Sebastian pushed his way through the blocks of foam, trying to get to the edge of the pit, and like a tortoise in pursuit, Mr. I followed, slowly getting closer and closer. He was evidently rather good at maneuvering through foam pits, and Sebastian briefly wondered how exactly a person developed that particular skill. Though, he realized, maybe he was doing that right now?

Finally Sebastian reached the pit edge and grabbed on for dear life . . . just as Mr. I managed to grab hold of his leg. The edge slipped from Sebastian's grasp and he was pulled under and into a yellow sea of blocks of foam. They smashed into his face, and seemed to fill his mouth and nose. He felt a surge of terror as he realized he was going to drown in a pit of foam blocks.

---

12 Though I still argue that the slowest chase happened at the Effervescent Bubble Gum Factory between Madame Effervescent and her ne'er-do-well son, who had attempted to burn down the factory for the insurance money. It concluded with a chase through a newly tarred street, resulting in all kinds of a sticky mess. But that's all beside the point.

He kicked with his free leg, trying to dislodge Mr. I's hand from his ankle, but the man's grip was actually very impressive. Or . . . maybe it wasn't. Sebastian suddenly found he was free, and he broke the surface of the foam pieces. He sucked in a huge breath of air and looked back to see Mr. I blinking hard, tossing his head this way and that, and his hair was all wet.

"Give me your hand!"

Sebastian had never been so happy to hear that voice in his life! Myrtle was standing above him, with what looked like a gun in one hand, the other stretched out toward him. He reached for it and she pulled as he pushed, and together they got him out of the pit. Sebastian quickly looked back and saw Mr. I slowly coming for them. Myrtle aimed her gun and fired again. Water streamed from the gun and hit him square in the face, causing him to snort and make strange guttural noises from behind his wired jaw, stopping him in his tracks.

"Let's go!" said Myrtle, and Sebastian was perfectly happy to obey that order. They ran down the hall and were making to turn right when they heard the sound of feet behind them. They looked back to see Mr. I not only free of the pit and reunited with his weapon, but chasing after them wearing a horrific grin on his face. Okay, it was probably more horrific because his jaw was wired shut and rusted bits of metal were caging his teeth; the grin itself was pretty average. Still. Not so great.

Sebastian, following close at Myrtle's always-very-competent heels, discovered they had immediately changed directions. Myrtle flung open a door and they darted inside. Ah, noted Sebastian, the giant map room. A room covered with nothing but giant maps except for the wall of windows that opened onto the street and the fireplace burning brightly at the far end. Another nifty feature? It only had one door. The one they'd just burst through.

Another dead end.

Sebastian looked at Myrtle, who seemed instantly to realize her mistake, and they made for the exit. But Sebastian found himself staring down the barrel of a gun as Mr. I stepped into the doorway.

➤ CHAPTER 25 ◄

In which we meet a pig
in a teeny hat. Again.

"Why is there a pig in here?" asked Evie.

"Why is he wearing a hat?" asked Catherine.

"Snort" was the pig in the teeny hat's reply.

Evie and Catherine finally took stock of the room before them. The pig in question was standing in a little pen in one corner, but it wasn't the only animal in the room. In a cage opposite were half a dozen green and blue budgies, all wearing teeny bowler hats and monocles. There was a large sandbox with three gerbils and two rats, the latter wearing teeny sunhats with flowers in them and the former wearing teeny baseball caps representing the three local teams.

There was another thud against the door, and Evie was pulled back to their emergency situation. "Quick! Let's grab something to block the door!" she called to Catherine.

But Catherine just stood there, a smile crossing her face.

"Catherine!" Evie called out, trying to pull her from her thoughts.

Catherine shook her head and walked toward the pig. It trotted away from her to the farthest corner of the pen and looked at her suspiciously. She stretched out her hand and made a soft sort of noise in the back of her throat. The pig continued to stare at her, and then slowly walked to her. With great trepidation it sniffed at her hand and then slowly rubbed its cheek up against it. Catherine raised the hand and gave the pig a long stroke along its back, and the pig seemed to rather enjoy it, moving in closer to her. She opened the pen and stood up. The pig stepped out and looked at her expectantly. She smiled. Evie wished Catherine would tell her what she was thinking; instead Evie just watched the woman with confusion.

Catherine went over to the birdcage next and

without pause opened the door. The birds flew out in a chaos of wings, flapping in a wide circle around the room, and then landed on her shoulders and head. The gerbils and rats, meanwhile, had already climbed out of their box and were standing at attention at her feet.

"Well, friends," said Catherine with a smile. "We could use your help."

There was a thud against the door again and everyone, human and beast alike, turned to see the wooden doorframe crack under the pressure.

"We could use a distraction," she explained.

Evie was pretty certain the animals didn't understand a word Catherine said, despite how intently they looked at her, though, yes, the rat in the straw hat with the pink flower did happen to nod just as she said it. Still. Evie assumed it was more that there was something in Catherine's tone that made the animals feel safe. Or want to do her proud. Or . . . something.

"What are you doing?" asked Evie as Catherine walked over to where she was standing by the door and placed her hand on the doorknob. The animals trotted behind her parade-style, except for the birds, which stayed perched on her person.

"Get ready to run when I say 'run,' " said Catherine.

"To where?" asked Evie, shifting the orb to her left hand.

"To the elevator; we need to get to the ground floor."

"But what about Sebastian?"

"If he's smart, he's also heading that way."

"He's smart," said Evie. *And I really hope he's okay,* she added to herself.

"You ready to run?" asked Catherine. Evie nodded, squeezing the orb tight. Catherine turned to the animals, which had all congregated at her feet. "And are you ready?" That rat nodded again, and now Evie thought maybe they did actually understand her.

Mr. K threw himself against the door once more, and the frame splintered even more. A gerbil wearing a Hamsters hockey team hat took a step to the right as a piece of wood fell to the floor.

"Little pig, little pig, let me come in!" Mr. K called, sounding out of breath on the other side of the door.

"That's your cue," said Evie to the pig in the teeny hat.

"Snort."

Catherine opened the door wide and looked at Mr. K with a smile. He stared back in horror. "Charge!" she cried, and the animals did just that as Mr. K cried out, "Not again!"

The budgies flew right at his face, and he stumbled backward, trying to wave them away as they pecked at him. The rats and gerbils, meanwhile, scurried up inside his pants legs, causing him to do what looked to be an elaborate jig.[13] But it was the pig who was the real star of the show. The pig had no particular grace or tact. But what it had was determination. And a very fine hat that made it feel really good about itself. When it was the pig's turn to charge, Evie was able to see from behind the flapping wings for just a moment. A look of complete fear had transformed Mr. K's face when he noticed the pig barreling toward him. With rats up his pants and budgies in his face, Mr. K stared in horror as the noble proud pig plowed into his shins and knocked him flat onto his back. Then, with a great sense of accomplishment, the pig climbed up onto Mr. K's torso and sat on his chest.

"Run!" said Catherine. Evie was so immersed in watching the animals that it took her a moment to realize that the time to take action had arrived.

She quickly followed Catherine, leaping over the fallen body of Mr. K as he continued to flail while firmly pinned by the pig. They arrived at the elevator and took it down to the main floor. Catherine dashed

---

[13] In fact, by sheer coincidence, he managed to dance the last sixteen bars of the "The Lilting Banshee."

out to the right, but Evie looked to the left. "Catherine!" she called.

Catherine stopped and turned. They watched as Sebastian darted into a room at the far end of the hall with Myrtle.

"Let's go!" said Evie, and Catherine nodded. As they rushed toward the door, Mr. I stepped out from a corridor to the right. Evie sucked in a quick breath and was readying herself to run in the opposite direction, but Mr. I didn't seem to notice that she and Catherine were directly behind him. He turned and made for the same door Sebastian and Myrtle had just fled through. Evie watched in terror as he sneaked up to the entrance, raising his gun.

"Oh no you don't," muttered Catherine. She unfurled her whip and drew her arm back, then, with an enormous heave, lashed out at Mr. I.

⤞CHAPTER 26⤝

In which there is much ado about maps.

Sebastian wasn't exactly sure what had happened. One moment he was staring down the barrel of a rather old-fashioned-looking gun. The next minute Mr. I had fallen face-first on the ground, hitting his head hard and losing consciousness, revealing Catherine holding a whip in her hand and Evie standing next to her holding a round golden ball. Catherine leapt over Mr. I's body and grabbed his gun.

"Where did the whip come from?" asked Sebastian.

"You're okay!" said Evie, rushing over to him.

"I am. And so are you." He smiled in pure relief and joy.

"Do you still have the key?" she asked.

He nodded.

Evie then turned to Myrtle. "Please," she said, "let us keep it and we'll take it away somewhere they'll never find it."

Myrtle looked at Catherine, then at Evie. "How can I trust you?"

There was only one logical answer to that, and Sebastian had it. "By trusting her," he said.

Myrtle snorted and then sighed as Catherine came over and said, "I know you don't approve. I know you don't like us. But something big is going on with Alistair. He's in danger. We need to help him. He asked us to protect the key, and he wouldn't have if it wasn't vitally important."

Sebastian agreed and approached Myrtle as well. "Yes! There must be a reason for that."

He looked at Catherine, who smiled at him. He turned to glance back at Evie.

"No one move," said Mr. K.

The cold metal of the knife's edge against her throat was shocking, the grip on her upper arm painfully tight. But those feelings were eclipsed by the expressions on the faces she saw before her. If she hadn't already felt scared enough, looking into the eyes of those who thought you were about to die was utterly and completely terrifying.

No one spoke for a good long while, and per Mr. K's instructions no one moved, either. It was a moment frozen in time. Evie wanted it to be over, and yet didn't. Because when the moment was over, what would become of her? She swallowed hard and fought back tears. This time she wouldn't cry. She wouldn't give this man the satisfaction.

"Good," said Mr. K. "Now listen carefully. I'm not an unreasonable person. I am more than willing to offer an exchange."

"Oh really?" asked Myrtle. She looked none too pleased, that was for sure. And Evie appreciated that.

"Really. It's quite simple. The girl's life for the key. And since we're all gathered here today, I'd also like Catherine Lind's piece of the map. Not bad terms, eh?" said Mr. K. He tightened his grip on Evie, which made her squeak in fear. "Meanwhile, I'll take this." He plucked the EM-7056 from Evie's hand so quickly she didn't have time to fight him for it.

Sebastian looked at Catherine and Myrtle, then back at Mr. K. Slowly he removed the key from his pocket and held it out in front of him. Evie didn't understand what he was doing. There was no way he was considering passing over the key. Surely that wasn't an option. She watched him stare hard at the piece of paper. Or was it?

Her fear blossomed now. She thought it had already reached its apex, but no, evidently that had been just phase one. It wasn't her life that mattered anymore. It was what was to happen with the key. And that decision rested in Sebastian's hands. Literally.

"Come on, boy, don't waste time, now. You too, Lind," said Mr. K.

Evie saw Catherine stiffen. Slowly, and clearly with great effort, she reached into her coat and withdrew her part of the map. She held it at her side for a moment, still thinking hard.

"Don't do it!" called out Evie, and Mr. K squeezed her arm so tightly, she was certain he was cutting off her circulation.

Catherine looked at Sebastian, and so did Evie. He was still staring at the key. He was thinking hard. Solving some problem. Trying to logic his way out of this situation. Probably trying to come up with the most effective . . .

No.

No.

Don't do it, Sebastian, Evie thought. *Please. Don't do what I think you're about to do.*

"Don't!" she called out. "Please don't."

"Come on, pass them over," said Mr. K.

Sebastian made eye contact with her. "I'm sorry," he whispered.

And he threw the key into the fireplace.

"No!" screamed Evie.

Mr. K let go of her arm as he lunged for the key, and she fell to the floor. As he flew at the fireplace,

Myrtle neatly knocked him in the back of the head with what looked like a water gun, and Mr. K fell hard to the floor.

Evie was on her feet in an instant and charging past Sebastian to the fireplace. She scrambled over the felled Mr. K. "No no no no no," she said, staring into flames. But it was too late. The fire had made short work of the key. There was nothing left of it but black ash.

She felt a warm hand on her back as she knelt in front of the fireplace. It was Sebastian. "I'm sorry . . . ," he said softly.

"Don't touch me!" she said, whipping around and flinging off his hand. How could he do it? He knew how much it mattered to her, to her grandfather. If the key was destroyed, then her grandfather's life was in peril. Sebastian knew that! How could he do this to her? She stood upright, and not knowing what to do, just knowing that she needed to get out of there, she bolted out of the room, tears streaming down her face.

Sebastian made to follow, utterly distraught at how upset his friend was. But Myrtle held him back. "Let me," said Catherine, and she left the room.

"I need to explain," he said, struggling against the old woman's strong grasp.

"Not now," replied Myrtle.

Sebastian felt desperate; he needed to talk to Evie. To explain why he'd done it. So she'd understand. So she'd forgive him.

"She needs to understand," he said.

"Not now, Sebastian, not now. Let her be upset. This isn't about you," said Myrtle.

"But it is, it's all about me. I can fix it . . . if I just explain logically. . . ."

"Sometimes, Sebastian, you can't just explain things. Even when we understand the logic, the feelings win out. You have to let people feel things."

"But it's so painful knowing I've hurt her like this." Sebastian realized only then that tears were streaming down his face.

"That's what happens sometimes. But as I said before, this isn't about you. It's about her. And you just have to feel the pain for now."

"I did it to help her," Sebastian said softly.

"Yes, you did," Myrtle answered. "And deep down she knows that."

Sebastian stopped trying to pull free and wiped his face.

"Come, come," said Myrtle, turning him around to face her. She brought him in for a hug, and he let her.

"I did it to save her life," he said into her shoulder.

"Of course you did. And she'll understand that."

He nodded into the woman's sweater and squeezed her tighter.

"Where are my animals?"

Sebastian broke out of the hug and turned to see Hubert holding a giant butterfly net. Behind him stood two animal control operatives wearing white hazmat suits and carrying two massive cages.

"What are you talking about, Hubert?" asked Myrtle with a sigh.

"They've been set free! All my animals! These gentlemen are trying to help me round them up!" The old man looked even more frazzled than usual.

"We'll help with that too," said Sebastian, and then he had a thought. "Hey, do you think those two animal control guys would mind taking away these men for us?" He gestured at the prostrate Mr. I and Mr. K in disgust.

Hubert looked at them for a moment and then nodded enthusiastically. "Of course. Of course, they're human, and human is a subspecies of animal, and they seem frightfully unpleasant. Have they had their shots?"

"Uh, well, Hubert, we can't actually do that . . . ," said one of the men.

"Can you at least take them to the police station? As a favor? To . . . to Hubert?" asked Sebastian.

"Yes! As a favor to me!" said Hubert enthusiastically.

The men looked at each other for a moment. "Okay, sure, Hubert. As a favor to you."

Hubert smiled, and with remarkable speed Mr. I and Mr. K were caged up and dragged off down the hall.

"That's that, then," said Myrtle, watching them go.

"That's that." Though Sebastian really didn't feel like anything was resolved, not really. Not at all.

"Come on," said Myrtle with a firm pat on his back. "Let's have a spot of tea."

>CHAPTER 27<

In which we come
to the end.

Evie lay on the soft deep-red quilted comforter and stared at the warm wooden ceiling. Silent tears spilled down her cheeks, and though she knew she should be grateful and happy, she wasn't sure how she could feel that. Slowly she pushed herself up to sitting and looked at her small room. It was a world apart from her old one at the Wayward School. Still small, but instead of claustrophobic, it was cozy, with its lush red and gold pillows, wooden armoire and desk, and large, sparkling-clean window that opened onto the leafy street below.

There was a knock on the door, and Evie hastily rubbed the tears from her face and stood up. She put her small suitcase on the bed and opened it. "Just un-packing!" she said loudly.

"Can I come in?"

It was Sebastian. Evie looked at the door for a moment and then with a sigh said, "Okay."

Sebastian opened the door and took a few tentative steps into the room.

"I didn't mean to interrupt," he said quietly.

"It's okay," she said. She couldn't look at him. Even though she knew he had only done what he'd thought was right, it still hurt too much. It was a full day later and it still stung like it had happened a moment ago.

"So this is neat," said Sebastian. "Uh. You getting to live at the society headquarters. Be their ward."

"Sure is," replied Evie. She grabbed the picture of her parents and placed it carefully on her bedside table.

"And you get to go to school here too. Get to be taught by the members and everything. Which should be amazing."

He was telling her things she already knew, awkwardly making small talk. Evie couldn't help feeling sorry for him. Just a little bit. He was so uncomfortable and was clearly feeling guilty.

"Hope so," she said, folding her sweater and then walking by Sebastian to her armoire and placing it inside. Finally she turned. He looked so sad—almost pathetic. "Sebastian, what do you want?"

He sighed and shook his head. "I just . . . I want to be friends again. I want you to forgive me."

"I do forgive you," she said, though the lump in her throat was growing.

"I mean really forgive me," he said, his voice cracking. "I mean, I just made what I thought was the logical choice."

Evie scoffed at that. "Yup, it was logical." It was. She couldn't think of anything else he could have done. But it didn't make it hurt any less. Yes, Sebastian had saved her life, but he'd placed her grandfather's in mortal peril. It didn't matter how much Catherine had promised when she'd chased her down the hall yesterday that they would find and rescue him. Evie knew she had failed her grandfather. Failed to protect the key, failed to protect him. And now the key was gone forever. "Look, Sebastian, this is hard, and I'm upset. But I do forgive you, and I'm sure in time I'll be less sad about this. We're still friends, I promise."

"Well, okay," said Sebastian. "But I want to explain why—"

"Sebastian, I don't want to hear it, okay? I get it. You thought you were saving my life, and you thought that by destroying the key all this would be done. It would be over. No more bad men hunting anyone down for their bits of maps and stuff. And I get it. You saved a lot of people, not just me, and you sacrificed one person for that. My grandfather. And right now that's all I can think about."

"But if you'll just let me—"

"Sebastian, seriously, now's not the time."

"Yes it is. I know people don't want me to explain, but I need to. The key—"

"Is not actually gone, is it?" The voice that spoke was unfamiliar, and both kids turned abruptly to stare at the doorway.

Standing there ever so casually was a slender man in a black leather jacket with a patch over one eye. He smiled as he walked into the room, closing the door behind him.

"Uh . . . who are you?" asked Sebastian, but Evie knew this wasn't the time for questions. It was the time for action.

"Help!" she screamed. "Help us!"

Her cry was drowned out by the sound of exploding glass. She covered her head as the window sent thousands of shards in their direction. When she looked up again, she saw Mr. I dangling outside the window holding on to a thick black cable. She turned, and the man in her doorway was holding Sebastian tightly, a pistol pointed at his temple. A reversal of sorts of what had happened the day before. Only this time Evie had nothing to sacrifice to save him like he had for her.

"Mr. I tells me you have a very impressive memory," said the man as he marched Sebastian over to the window. Evie was working on instinct now and lunged at him, but the man easily pushed her back to the floor. Her hand landed on a piece of glass and she winced in pain.

"How could he tell you anything?" said Sebastian, struggling hard against the man.

"He can't talk, but he can sign. And he can hear. And he overheard you at the zoo," said the man as he hoisted Sebastian up and held him out the window. Mr. I reached out to grab him.

"Stop it! What are you doing!" yelled Evie over what she realized was a loud whirring sound coming from outside.

"Your little friend *is* the key," said the man, handing over the still-struggling Sebastian and stepping over the ledge.

Evie sat in shock and stared at him as he smiled one more time. Of course. Sebastian's memory. His perfect photographic memory. He knew what was written on the key. He had destroyed it because he remembered it.

And then the man stepped out the window and leapt for the cable. Evie was on her feet immediately and over to the window. Sebastian, Mr. I, and the man were slowly being raised into a large black helicopter hovering over the building.

"Sebastian!" she cried out.

"It's okay! They can't hurt me! They need what's in my brain. Not even a neurosurgeon could get that for them!" Sebastian smiled at her, but she knew he was just doing it to make her feel better.

As he was drawn higher and higher up, Evie called after him, "I'll save you! I'll find you and I'll save you! I promise!"

But she didn't think Sebastian heard that, and all she could do was watch as he got smaller and smaller and then vanished into the helicopter.

She dashed back into her room and out into the hall, almost falling over the pig in a teeny hat. It looked up at her, and somehow its expression made her all the more resolute. This time she wouldn't fail. This time she would absolutely save him. And she ran down the hall for help, the pig close on her heels.

➤ EPILOGUE ◄

Kidnapped, or ruminations from within a helicopter.

Sebastian sat squashed between Mr. I and Mr. K, being stared at by the one eye of the third man sitting across from him. He was being taken to who knows where, the only thing keeping him alive an accident of birth that had for some reason given him a remarkably interesting memory.

A panic attack was quickly coming upon him. His mind was racing a mile a minute—he could barely keep track of all his thoughts, which was unusual for him. He got mere glimpses. Mere flashes.

Fear. Terror.

What's happening?

Is this a dream?

More fear. More terror.

But also something else.

Guilt.

It rushed through his brain so quickly, he barely noticed it, but his gut felt it. His gut reached out and grabbed it and held it fast.

Because certainly this was a scary experience. He'd never before been in so much danger. But worse than that for poor pragmatic, logical, level-headed Sebastian, it appeared that a part of him found this all rather thrilling.

And he really oughtn't be feeling that way, right?

Right?

Sebastian leaned back in his seat and looked out the window trying to calm himself down, taking in long, deep breaths. The sun glowed bright orange behind a dense skyline of skyscrapers, and he watched as the helicopter flew over and beyond them and toward the great unknown, which currently looked like farm fields and apple orchards. But metaphorically, you know . . . the future. It was unknown.

Thus ends our tale for now.

Don't you hate stories that end in cliff-hangers? They are just so . . .

➤ ACKNOWLEDGMENTS ◄

My fantastic agent, Jess Regel, who never ceases to amaze me with her unwavering support and inspiring pep talks, along with everyone else at Foundry Literary.

My tireless editor, Krista Marino, who meticulously went over every element of this book as much as I did, and everyone at Delacorte Press.

Illustrator Matt Rockefeller, who somehow managed to bring my crazy brain manifestations to life.

My family.

My friends.

My two guys: Scott the human and Atticus the cat.

And my mom and dad—whom I love more than words can say, but evidently I did have the words to say it.

Thank you so much for all the support, sanity checks, and hugs.

I acknowledge you all.

Things are just getting interesting,
aren't they?
Find out what happens
to Sebastian and Evie next in

THE RECKLESS RESCUE

ADRIENNE KRESS is a writer and an actress born and raised in Toronto. She is the daughter of two high school English teachers, and credits them with inspiring her love of both writing and performing. She has a cat named Atticus, who unfortunately despises teeny hats. Look for her online at AdrienneKress.com and on both Twitter and Instagram at @AdrienneKress.